A CANDLELIGHT ROMANCE

Candlelight Romances

568 SPANISH MASQUERADE, *Jane Peart*
569 THE PEACOCK BED, *Joanne Marshall*
574 TENDER IS THE TOUCH, *Anne Shore*
575 ENTWINED DESTINIES, *Rosalind Welles*
576 DARK PARADISE, *Berrie Davis*
577 THE FLOWERS OF DARKNESS, *Elisabeth Barr*
582 JOY RUNS HIGH, *Tilly Armstrong*
583 PRECIOUS PIRATE, *Esther Boyd*
584 TOUCHED BY FIRE, *Mary Lee Stanford*
585 THE WEDDING JOURNEY, *Marjorie Eatock*
590 LOVE IN THE WILDS, *Suzanne Roberts*
591 FORBIDDEN BLESSING, *Lucy Casselman*
592 MORNING ROSE, EVENING SAVAGE, *Amii Lorin*
598 ISLAND LOVESONG, *Louise Bergstrom*
599 EAST TO PARADISE, *Jacqueline Hacsi*
600 DARE TO LOVE, *Candice Arkham*
601 THE MASK OF LOVE, *Katherine Court*
606 COME NOVEMBER, *Virginia Myers*
607 A LOVE TO REMEMBER, *Ida Hills*
608 THE SEARCHING HEART, *Anne Shore*
609 WICKLOW CASTLE, *Mary Hanson*
614 A FLIGHT FOR DREAMERS, *Jane Converse*
615 TO SEIZE THE RAINBOW, *Jo Calloway*
616 LOVE'S SWEET SURRENDER, *Arlene Hale*
617 SHADOWS OF THE HEART, *Lorena McCourtney*
622 COUNTERFEIT HONEYMOON, *Julia Anders*
623 HEART ON HOLIDAY, *Elaine Fowler Palencia*
624 BALI BREEZES, *Esther Boyd*
628 DAZZLED BY DIAMONDS, *Phyllis Kuhn*
629 THE BECKONING HEART, *Alyssa Morgan*
630 THE CHAPERONE, *Ethel E. Gordon*
634 HIBISCUS LAGOON, *Dorothy Dowdell*
635 LASTING LOVE, *Antonia Blake*
636 PORTRAIT OF LOVE, *Jean Hager*
640 PARADISE ISLE, *Jacqueline Hacsi*
641 LOVE ISLAND, *Barbara Max*
642 THE TREACHEROUS HEART, *Helen Nuelle*
646 PERILOUS WATERS, *Jane Blackmore*
647 HALF-HEART, *Amanda Preble*
648 THE KINDRED SPIRIT, *Ginger Chambers*

PORTRAIT *in* SHADOWS

Jane Peart

A CANDLELIGHT ROMANCE

Published by
Dell Publishing Co., Inc.
1 Dag Hammarskjold Plaza
New York, New York 10017

ISBN: 0-440-16693-4

Printed in the United States of America
First printing—May 1981

PORTRAIT
in
SHADOWS

CHAPTER 1

As I left San Francisco the sun was just burning off the early morning fog and washing the city with a pristine radiance. I drove through the quiet streets not yet jammed with commuter traffic and took the coast route to Monterey. Driving along the nearly deserted freeway, I thought what a strange role fate plays in our lives. Because of two totally unexpected events the whole course of my summer had been changed.

The first one had been a drastic blow—my engagement to young Dr. Doug Staley and the European honeymoon his parents had promised him, both wiped out in one short evening. For Doug I had turned down a year's scholarship in Paris the year before. If I would wait until he finished his internship, he had begged me, we could go together.

Then four months ago he had told me awkwardly that there was someone else and that maybe we were not meant for each other after all.

"I don't think it would have worked with us, Cam. I'm a doctor, and artists and doctors live in two different worlds. They see things differently, want different things out of life—"

I listened numbly, searching for the real reason beyond the excuse which seemed too weak to end a relationship that had lasted two years without any apparent problems. Hurt and shocked I pretended to accept it. What else could I do?

Somehow I got through the rest of my year of teaching art at an exclusive girls' school in Marin. I survived by doing all the cliché things those articles in women's magazines tell you to do to get over an unhappy love affair. I tried a new look, a new hobby, new interests. While nothing provided a complete answer, all helped. The short haircut was more becoming than the old long one, tennis improved my figure, and meeting new men who seemed to find me interesting was good for my bruised ego.

Gradually I convinced myself that in spite of what had happened, I was still reasonably attractive, talented, popular with my students, and accepted by my fellow teachers. At twenty-five I had my whole life ahead of me, even if it did not include marriage to Doug.

At the end of the spring term, I packed my VW with painting equipment, planning to start out on a vagabond summer, traveling down the coast, stopping wherever I wanted to sketch and paint, and filling my portfolio with new work—enough, hopefully, for a show the next fall.

Then I received the phone call from my Aunt Mim that changed the direction of my summer.

"I'm so glad I caught you, dear. I was afraid you might have already left and I did so want to reach you," she said, then proceeded to tell me about the reception she was having the next day for Justin Bradford, the author.

"It really was quite a stroke of luck getting him," Aunt Mim continued. "He's just back from his chalet in Switzerland and finishing up a promotional tour for his latest book. The publicity department of his publishing house had him lined up for all sorts of talk shows and interviews, plus appearing at four different bookstores to meet people and sign autographs. However, when I told them I could arrange to have just as many people here—well, they were delighted and so was he! That kind of thing can be exhausting and to have one appearance do the work of four was most welcome. Now, you will come, won't you, dear?"

I was reluctant. I disliked the idea of postponing my trip, the thought of which had sustained me through the dreariest spring of my life. But how often did you have the chance to meet the author of several best sellers? In the end I told Aunt Mim I'd be there.

As I drove into the city from my apartment in Mill Valley on the afternoon of the autograph party, I found I was actually looking forward to it. I loved visiting my aunt's big Victorian house in San Francisco. It had been in her husband's family for four generations and still had some of the original opulent furnishings brought west by ship in the early days of the Gold Rush.

When I walked in the front door I saw there was already a crowd milling through the huge center hall, flowing from one twin parlor to the other, and spilling out into the walled garden beyond.

At first I saw no sign of Aunt Mim. Then I caught a glimpse of her attempting to get a group of ladies, all clutching copies of Justin Bradford's latest book, into some kind of orderly line. Standing in front of the massive marble fireplace behind her was a man I recognized immediately as the author himself.

He looked just like the pictures on the back of his book jackets, exactly how you imagine a writer should look but seldom does. He was tall and ruggedly handsome with wavy gray hair, deep-set eyes, a heroic nose, and a jutting jaw. He wore a tweed sports coat with a silk scarf knotted at his throat, and he held a pipe in one hand.

My glance was then drawn to the young woman beside him. I remembered my aunt's saying just before we'd hung up, "Oh, by the way, he's practically on his honeymoon, and his bride will be along."

My first thought was that she must be at least twenty years younger than he, my second was that she would be wonderful to paint. Her profile turned toward him was cameolike. She had beautiful facial planes, porcelain skin, and a mist of blue-black hair falling in soft waves to her shoulders.

Then Aunt Mim saw me and waved me forward. Excusing myself, I passed through the cluster of fans and, when

I reached her side, she stage-whispered, "We'll take a break in a minute, then I'll introduce you to Justin. He saw your portrait of my twins in the hall and liked it tremendously, and asked who had painted them. When I told him my niece, Cameron Forrest, he said he'd like to talk to you about painting Dortha, his wife!" She squeezed my arm excitedly.

I found my way to the punch bowl, helped myself, then wandered back out to the hall to take a look at the painting I'd done of my cousins the year before. Anne and Adele were identical twins, and it had been quite a challenge while painting them together to capture each one's individuality. I felt it was one of my better efforts, and Aunt Mim and Uncle Ted had been delighted.

It was some time before Aunt Mim could maneuver her celebrity guest away from his adoring fans and get us together in a quiet corner for a chance to talk.

"I've wanted to have Dortha's portrait painted for some time now," Justin said. "I'm really impressed with the sensitivity of your work. I think you have the style that would do justice to Dortha's ethereal quality. Do you think you'd be interested?"

Interested was hardly the word. It was the kind of opportunity a portraitist, especially one just starting out, always hopes will come along. However, it wasn't until the crowd had finally all left that we got down to discussing the details of my new commission.

"I want you to come as soon as possible, after we get settled at Gull's Glen. This is a very special time in our lives, and I want Dortha painted in all her fresh loveliness, just as she is now, before anything happens to change her—" He broke off abruptly. "How soon can you arrange to come?"

I think even then I was somewhat puzzled by Justin's intensity about having Dortha's portrait painted, but it was only much later that I realized it was actually an obsession. At the time I never imagined what accepting his invitation would involve, I simply answered his question.

"I usually require at least five sittings for a full figure portrait," I said, "but sometimes I take a day or two to do some preliminary drawings. Especially if I don't know my subject."

"Time is no problem," he responded. "Take however long you must. You'll have one of the guest cottages; work at your own speed. We'll be there until I get my next book well under way. Later I may have to do more research, but until then we'll remain at Gull's Glen. Noplace else affords me the peace and privacy I need to get a book started."

After the Bradfords left by a limousine, provided by Justin's publishers, to be driven back to their Nob Hill hotel, Aunt Mim bubbled with enthusiasm.

"It could be the turning point in your career!" Aunt Mim said over and over. "Think of the opportunity of painting the portrait of the wife of a famous writer like Justin Bradford. The people he must know! The people they entertain—they'll all see the portrait, and who knows what doors will open for you afterward!"

Although I did not have Aunt Mim's unlimited optimism about becoming internationally known by doing Dortha Bradford's portrait, I did have to admit it was a turning point. It had been so long since I'd felt enthusiastic about anything that it definitely helped to have something to look forward to again.

That evening as I drove back to Mill Valley I reassessed my summer plans. With the money from the Bradford commission I could extend my travels, maybe even go to Mexico where I could live cheaply and paint. Maybe I wouldn't have to go back to my teaching job in the fall. I felt a thrill of excitement about all the possibilities this one portrait might bring me.

The next Sunday there was an article and interview with Justin Bradford in the Scene-Arts section of the newspaper. I read it with interest. There were pictures of him and Dortha and of their home on the Monterey peninsula. Among other things it said, "Justin Bradford produces a novel about every two years. Most of them manage to reach the top of the bestseller list within weeks of publication. Most are written, at least in first draft, at his Big Sur home, Gull's Glen, built of native stone and redwood, perched on a soaring cliff with a sweeping view of the Pacific from almost every window."

A few weeks after our meeting I found a note from Justin in my mailbox. It was on smooth gray stationery addressed with a broad tip pen in a bold, slanting hand. It read:

> We're home, thank God, at last! We finished the last of our personal appearances in Seattle and came straight here. I was a total wreck, and it took me some days to feel myself again. The ocean is seductively beckoning me away from my desk, where I should be working this morning. But right now, I don't know if I shall ever write another book if I have to go on tour promoting it! Please come quickly or you may miss our best weather. Dortha is having second thoughts about having her portrait painted, but I have insisted. Let us know when to expect you.

Since my VW had been packed for weeks, it only took me a few more days to get ready to leave. I'd subleased my apartment for three months, so I spent the weekend before with Aunt Mim in San Francisco. I discussed Justin's note with her, expressing some anxiety about Dortha's changed attitude.

"I only hope her reluctance is temporary," I sighed. "There's nothing harder than painting someone who doesn't want to be painted."

I thought about that as I drove south and decided there

was no use worrying about something that might be all smoothed out by the time I got there.

CHAPTER 2

I decided to stop in Carmel first before traveling farther down the coast since Gull's Glen was only another hour's drive, and I'd never been to this picturesque little town.

Carmel, in spite of its growth in recent years, has managed to retain its uniqueness. The winding streets, with sidewalks built to accommodate the trees that shade them, dozens of small shops, art galleries, gift, book, and clothing stores, and boutiques all lend their own special charm.

Although I'd never been there myself, I'd heard so much about Carmel, I was anxious to explore it. I had to make three complete tours of the streets before I located a place to park. Lucky to have a tiny car, I thought, as I maneuvered my VW into a small space between a Mercedes and a Porsche. Carmel is a very high income-area, I reminded myself.

I needed no reminders when I examined the price tags in one of the dress shops I browsed through. Those prices were hardly suited to a teacher's salary, but it was fun to fantasize wearing the clothes. The other stores and shops were equally fascinating, and I wandered in and out of a dozen gift, pottery, and jewelry stores. After an hour or more I was almost dizzy from looking and walking. I'd find an art supply store, get the things I needed, then find a place to eat lunch, I decided.

I didn't have far to go. Turning the corner into a side

street, I spotted an attractive wooden sign, beautifully hand-lettered.

ARTISTS' SUPPLIES, FRAMING, GALLERY

Outside were two cedar planter boxes, bright with nasturtiums and royal blue lobelia; there were double bay display windows on either side of a Dutch door in which were two lovely seascapes, handsomely framed.

As I pushed open the door, a bell above it jangled merrily. Inside was a Franklin stove and an old brick floor. A doorway to one side was marked GALLERY. Behind a counter of old, polished wood a dark-haired young man looked up and smiled at my approach.

"Hi. Can I help you find anything?" he asked.

I mentioned a certain brand of sketch pad I liked to use for my preliminaries with pen and ink and wash, and he came out from around the counter to show me where they were stacked by size.

He was about medium height, slim but well-built, with nice shoulders. He wore a navy V-neck sweater and gray cords and had nice, even features, lively blue eyes, and the nicest smile I'd ever noticed in a man. His teeth were very white and straight against his tan skin.

I picked out a couple of sketch books, then started to look for some new brushes. I always liked to have extras besides my old favorites. I took a long time selecting them, but he was very patient. When I had everything I wanted, he took them all over to the counter to tally and package.

"Looks like you're planning to do a lot of work. Are you staying in Carmel long?" he asked.

"As long as it takes," I replied, adding, "I'm here on a commission to paint a portrait."

"Oh?" he said, an unspoken question in his tone.

"I'm doing a portrait of Dortha Bradford."

"Why, that's great! A lot of artists would envy you a

commission like that. After all, Justin Bradford's famous. It can't do your career any harm getting that kind of recognition."

He rang up the sale, took my credit card, and turned the sales slip around for my signature before he commented, "Cameron Forrest. I'll have to remember that. You'll probably be famous someday."

I felt my face get hot. I was embarrassed. It probably sounded like the worst kind of name dropping on my part to have told a perfect stranger about the commission. I hoped this nice man wouldn't get the wrong impression of me. At the same time I wondered why that seemed suddenly important. Quickly I rushed to my own defense, blurting out, "It's really my first big commission. I'm a teacher right now, but I do want to do portraits and this is a good start."

His smile widened, and he seemed to look at me with new interest.

"Actually I'm a little nervous about it," I confided, not knowing why I was telling all this to a stranger.

He nodded. "I can understand that," he said. "I know a few artists." He indicated the archway leading to the gallery. "Even the best, the most established artists, have those feelings when they're starting a special project. It shows you have respect for your craft."

That made me feel better and I smiled.

"By the way," he added, "I'm Jeff Maxwell, owner, framer, general flunky here. Have you known the Bradfords long?" he asked, as he handed me my package.

"Not really. I just met them last month. Do you know them?"

"Well, of course, everyone around here knows Justin. He's a familiar figure five months out of the year—that is, he used to be. After the tragedy he went abroad . . ."

I frowned. "The tragedy?"

"You don't know about—" He paused. "You did know

he'd been married before? That the lady you're painting is the second Mrs. Bradford? Maybe I shouldn't have brought it up, but I just assumed everyone knew. It was in all the papers a few years ago."

I shook my head. "I was at college back east a few years ago," I said. "I don't know anything about a tragedy connected with Justin Bradford."

Just then the bell over the store door jangled, announcing the arrival of another customer. Jeff said in a low voice, "Can you wait a few minutes? Maybe since I've gone this far, I should tell you the rest."

My curiosity was aroused, so while Jeff went to wait on the customer, I wandered into the gallery to have a look.

The gallery was as tastefully done as the shop. The paintings were beautifully framed, lighted, and hung, with enough space so that each one was shown to its best advantage. My respect for Jeff Maxwell rose. Obviously he appreciated artists and their work and was in the right business.

I glanced at my watch. I really should have been on my way to Gull's Glen. I had told the Bradfords to expect me early in the afternoon. Besides, I felt a little uneasy discussing my future employers with someone I'd just met, even someone as nice as Jeff Maxwell seemed to be.

The customer, a middle-aged woman with wildly hennaed hair, bizarrely dressed like someone's version of a hip teen-ager, was taking an inordinately long time selecting her purchases. At one point Jeff glanced over at me with raised eyebrows, signaling his helplessness to speed up the transaction.

I walked back into the shop. The woman was still procrastinating over her selections. I waved to Jeff and said, "I'll see you another time."

I thought he looked disappointed, but his nod told me he understood. I felt sure I would see him again when I came into Carmel. And I wasn't sure I wanted to hear about the tragedy at Gull's Glen.

I found a charming little restaurant to have a sandwich and coffee. Then, resisting the temptation to spend any more time looking around the fascinating town, I went straight to my car to start the last part of my trip.

The area through which I now began driving was ruggedly beautiful. The farther down the coast I got, the more primitive the landscape became. On one side were the windblown hills colorful with golden poppies and purple lupine, on the other, cliffs that dropped sheerly down to where waves exploded against the jagged rocks. The sunny sky and the blue ocean seemed to merge. My mood became carefree. I began to feel that I was on the brink of a great adventure.

Less than fifteen minutes later the sky began to darken noticeably. Clouds formed a leaden canopy overhead and a light rain began to mist my windshield. This sudden change altered my lightheartedness, and I started watching anxiously for the turnoff Justin had said led to the private road to Gull's Glen. It was a small sign, he had written, and only the forewarned would be able to spot it.

He had drawn a rough sketch of a gull in flight to represent the sign I was to look for, adding, "Obviously I'm a better writer than artist, but I think you'll recognize it when you see it."

Only five or six miles farther on, I saw a crude wooden sign with the symbol. I braked quickly and made a sharp right into what seemed to be dense woods. Then I came upon a hurricane link fence. I had to get out to push the gate, open enough for me to nose my little car through, then in low gear inch up a steep, narrow, rutted road.

Justin, it seemed, went to great lengths to insure his privacy. As I went up the torturously winding road, I saw ragged rhododendrons and wild lilac growing in profusion on either side. Finally the tunnellike atmosphere created by the overhang of trees ended and in the clearing just ahead I saw the house silhouetted against the pewter-gray sky.

It was, as it had been described, a starkly architected building of stone and timber in a cluster of Monterey pines and cedars. Beyond I could see the ocean stretching endlessly.

For one moment as I drew to a stop in front, all my feelings of excitement were replaced by a sense of depressing isolation so swift and heavy that I felt suddenly overwhelmed.

I had no time to throw off this crushing weight and try to regain my former feeling of expectancy, because my attention was diverted by the sound of dogs barking frantically. I guessed my arrival had been announced. In another minute Justin Bradford strode out onto the deck of the house, followed by two large Weimaraners, the gray ghost dogs of legend and folklore.

CHAPTER 3

Justin was smiling broadly as he came toward me. He looked even handsomer than I remembered, with his newly acquired tan. He wore an Irish fisherman's knit sweater and tan slacks, and he greeted me heartily.

"Miss Forrest, it's good to see you. Glad you made it all right. We're difficult to find, but as I hope you'll agree, our seclusion is well worth it. Come in, come in. My sister-in-law, Bianca, has been waiting to meet you."

He opened the car door and helped me out in a courtly manner. His hand firmly under my elbow, we went up the shallow terrace steps. We had just reached the top when a tall, slender woman appeared in the curved arch of the massive front door.

"Ah, Bianca, there you are!" Justin greeted her. "Here

is Miss Forrest, the artist we've been expecting." He turned back to me and said, "This is the indispensable chatelaine of Gull's Glen, my first wife's sister, Bianca Matthews."

I was momentarily taken back at the identifying introduction. It startled me that his former wife's sister still lived at the home to which he had just brought his second bride. I tried not to show my surprise at this unusual circumstance as I shook hands with Bianca.

I was intrigued by her exotic looks. Her age was indeterminate, as her face was virtually unlined, but I assumed she must be in her forties. Her hair was a rich auburn with a few strands of silver that only served to dramatize the way it was waved back from her pale, triangular face. She wore a long woven skirt in earth colors, a knit top, and several interesting gold chains around her neck. Her eyes were greenish and accentuated with shadow and liner, but she wore no other visible make-up. Her words of greeting were gracious enough, but I was immediately aware of an underlying coldness in her welcome, and when her cool, thin hand pressed mine, I felt chilled.

"You must be tired from your drive," Justin said heartily. "Let me offer you a drink or perhaps a glass of sherry."

Before I even had a chance to answer, Bianca cut in sharply, "Justin, I'm sure Miss Forrest would rather get settled first. Freshen up after her long trip. Besides, I've already told Rachel to take a tea tray down to Miss Forrest's cottage. That will be far more refreshing and reviving than an alcoholic beverage, which is, of course, a depressant. Don't you agree, Miss Forrest?" Although she was speaking to me directly, it seemed more a factual statement than a question. "Besides, Justin, I am sure you haven't decided to do away with the cocktail hour which is only two hours from now!"

There was such a note of sarcasm in her tone that I couldn't help but glance at Justin to see how he was reacting to his sister-in-law's officious behavior.

But he seemed to be taking her intervention calmly enough. He gave a good-natured shrug and said, "Well, fine, then. Miss Forrest, I'll leave you in Bianca's capable charge and see you later."

"Come along, Miss Forrest," Bianca said, leading the way back out onto the front porch. "You can drive right to your cottage. Just follow the driveway along the side of the house as far as it goes, then you'll see a small, rustic bridge over the stream that flows through the property. Beyond that are three guest cottages. Yours is the first one. I'll take the footpath along the ocean and meet you there," she said and gave me a slight smile that never reached her eyes.

I eased the car slowly past the house and along a winding road, hardly wider than a path that seemed to lead into a thick forest. When I first saw the row of small cottages, I was immediately reminded of the illustrations from my childhood storybook of the seven dwarfs' home in *Snow White*. Each cottage was charming and imaginative, with latticed casement windows and wrought-iron hinges on the red doors.

The Elizabethan architecture of the little guest houses was in sharp contrast to the modern design of the main house. When I remarked on this to Bianca, who was waiting for me on the doorstep of the first one, she replied archly, "Oh, the house is Justin's Frank Lloyd Wright facsimile. A disciple of Wright's designed it and it's Justin status symbol. But these—" she gestured to the three cottages "—were all Rosalind's idea. My sister was a well-known Shakespearean actress before her marriage, you know, and was quite steeped in everything pertaining to that period."

I was a little chilled by Bianca's contemptuous tone of voice when speaking of Justin. It puzzled me. If there was hostility between them, why did she remain here and, more to the point, why did he tolerate her presence?

Inside, the cottage was even more delightful. There was

a stone fireplace with a comfortable couch and two easy chairs placed cozily in front of it. A round coffee table stood in the center of the room with a bowl of fruit and a brass container of shaggy purple asters on it. Issues of several popular magazines were fanned out on top. On the other side of the room was a floor-to-ceiling window with a panoramic view of the ocean.

"Oh, this is marvelous!" I said with genuine pleasure. "I hadn't realized I could see the ocean from here. Coming back here through the woods, I had the impression we were going away from the sea."

"The entire property is set on a T-shaped cliff above the cove. That is why from almost any vantage point one can see, hear, or smell the sea," Bianca answered.

"Let me show you the rest of the cottage so that you'll feel comfortable," she continued. "It is really self-contained. We like our guests to have privacy, so there is a small kitchen behind that half-bookcase there. The cabinets and tiny refrigerator are stocked with a few supplies —coffee, milk, juice, and other things. I believe most people like to be able to at least have a cup of coffee in the morning. We serve an English-style buffet breakfast at the main house at which guests can help themselves to something heartier if they like, but don't feel obligated. I'm sure you'll want to set your own schedule." She moved gracefully across the room and opened a door. "In here is the bedroom and adjoining bath. I think you'll find everything you need. So I'll leave you now. Rachel will be along with your tea tray presently."

She started toward the door, then paused with her hand on the knob, and said, "Someone will come down for you about six. Justin likes the little ritual of pre-dinner cocktails, although I—you see, I was educated and spent many years in Europe and I find this American custom rather—" She halted as if to avoid saying anything that might sound critical of Justin. "By the way, the fog is coming in rapidly, I notice, so I have to warn you—if you are so inclined—not to take the path along the seawall, not until you've been shown it, as it is rather narrow and slippery in bad weather and a sheer drop down treacherous cliffs. If you should slip—" She suddenly shuddered, and I saw a fleeting expression on her face, as if something frightening had just flashed into her mind. She quickly regained her composure.

"Incidentally," she continued, "we dress very casually here. I won't change for dinner, so you can judge for yourself what you'll be most comfortable wearing. Of course Dortha might—but then she dresses for Justin, still very much the bride," she finished, with a touch of cynicism in her voice.

The appearance of a middle-aged maid in a blue and white uniform at the cottage door changed her line of thought. Bianca turned and said, "Here's Rachel now with your tea. Rachel, this is Miss Forrest." When the maid had set down the tray and gone out, Bianca spoke again. "I forgot to mention that Justin's two teen-age children are here now, too. They've only recently come home from boarding school." She hesitated, as if searching for the right words. "They are rather unpredictable, to say the least. Aaron is sixteen, Olivia nearly fourteen, a difficult age." Bianca pursed her lips in thought before continuing. "I don't know whether Justin has prepared you for how isolated we are here. We rarely have company anymore, and it may be somewhat dreary for a young woman your age, who is used to an active social life."

"Miss Matthews, I've come to do a job," I said. "To paint Dortha's portrait. A portrait requires a great deal of work and concentration. Besides, it is so beautiful here, I'm sure I'll find plenty to keep me happy when I'm not working."

Bianca frowned slightly and said rather doubtfully, "I do hope so. Well, good-bye for now. I'll see you at dinner." With that she went out and closed the cottage door.

After Bianca left, I walked all around the cottage, inspecting every corner of what was to be my living quarters for the next few weeks. It was a perfect gem of a little house, I thought, ideal for an artist.

I went over to the picture window and looked out. The storm that had threatened during the afternoon was still gathering. Heavy, dark clouds moved restlessly across the sky; waves hurled themselves angrily in great fronds of white spray upon the rocks below.

Suddenly I shivered. For some reason I was aware of an indefinable uneasiness.

I thought of the strange situation up at the main house—the curious trio of Justin, his new wife, and the sister of his dead wife. His children were there, too, I remembered. I wondered how they had reacted to their beautiful stepmother, hardly much older than they were themselves. And what kind of a tragedy had Jeff Maxwell meant when he talked about what happened at Gull's Glen?

I turned away from the window and back to the cozy room. Before she left, the maid had lighted the fire, and it had begun to glow pleasantly. I drew up a chair in front of it, poured myself a cup of the steaming, fragrant tea, and tried to forget that moment of shivery disquiet.

CHAPTER 4

For dinner that first evening I chose a tailored white silk blouse and a colorfully patterned long skirt, hoping they would be appropriate. I was just putting on silver hoop earrings when promptly at six there was a knock at the cottage door.

I opened it to Justin, looking handsome in a plaid jacket and ruffled shirt. Not as casual as Bianca suggested, I thought. He held out his arm, and we started out on the path to the main house.

It was getting dark and the thickness of the woods intensified the gloom. Justin switched on the flashlight he was carrying and its powerful beam illuminated the way.

"Have you started your new book yet, Mr. Bradford," I asked.

His half-groan hinted his probable answer. "Please call me, Justin, won't you?" he said. "And no. To my own and my publisher's despair, the book is going badly. I've only the bare outline and a few notes and am having the devil of a time coming up with more than a paragraph or two a day. Of course, it takes a while to get back to a regular schedule of writing after one has been away from it for some time. And then, these have not been what you might call routine days since we came back here. My children. I suppose Bianca told you that Aaron and Olivia arrived only a few days after Dortha and I got here—earlier than I expected them. You know how it is with young people around, especially when they're restless and not adjusting —" He broke off to warn, "Watch your step here. The path narrows and the rains have washed away the protective rock seawall. I must have that rebuilt. It's things like that, too, that keep me from my work. When you've been gone several months, you find so many things that need doing around a place. Sometimes I think we should have done what Dortha wanted to do—just travel about Europe for a while instead of coming back here. But there's something about this place, this particular stretch of coast. It's like an ancient sea siren to me, I guess. It keeps up its haunting cry and I succumb. But—" Again he broke off to caution me, "Be careful, now. The rain has made this path damnably slippery."

As we neared the house, lights shining from the tall windows made Justin's flashlight unnecessary. The front door opened as if from a signal, and Bianca stood in the doorway.

"What kept you?" she asked. "I thought perhaps you two got lost along the way."

"We took the sea path," Justin answered shortly. "You know how treacherous it is after rain." I thought he sounded a bit irritated, but if he was at all annoyed, it vanished immediately at the approach of Dortha behind Bianca. "Darling!" he greeted her. "How lovely you look. Here is Miss Forrest, who will, no doubt, be able to put it all on her canvas."

If anything, Dortha Bradford seemed even more beautiful than I had remembered her, I thought, as she came forward, both graceful hands extended to welcome me.

"So nice to see you again, Miss Forrest," she said in her breathless, little-girl voice. Justin put his arm around her shoulder and kissed her cheek.

Dortha was dressed in a fashion to match Justin's—her long, flowing caftanlike dress of chiffon in blending shades of blue and green. At close range, she seemed a little more fragile than I had recalled, paler and more slender. But she was still exquisite, and the thought of painting her excited me.

"Come along, ladies, let's go into the living room and have our drinks," suggested Justin genially.

Perhaps because of its rustic exterior, I was not prepared for the elegance of the interior of the Bradford mansion. I should have guessed that a man of Justin's taste and sophistication would live in such an environment. The furniture was French, the other art objects, paintings, and accoutrements showed a wide diversity of source and origin. It was not a room that looked as though a professional decorator had been called in, but it had a unified atmosphere that was not unlike a stage setting.

"Now, what is everyone drinking or should I serve the specialty of the house?" Justin asked, rubbing his hands together jovially.

Dortha laughed and said to me in a mock conspiratorial

tone of voice, "That means he wants to fix his own concoction, so why don't we humor him?"

"That will be just fine for me," I smiled.

"Just a small sherry for me, Justin, please," said Bianca in her cool, superior tone.

I shot a quick glance at Bianca, who looked slightly bored, and thought, aha, she isn't going to enter into the light mood Dortha and Justin were projecting. Why not? I wondered. Maybe it was hard for her to be the third member on an extended honeymoon. That in itself was strange, especially since her relationship to Justin was from the past, from another marriage. Could Bianca resent the fact of Justin's remarriage, his new bride? I couldn't tell. There was no overt sign of any hostility in the polite, civilized conversation the three engaged in while Justin mixed the drinks at a refectory table to one side of the fireplace. And was it *Miss* Matthews or *Mrs.* Matthews? Justin had made no indication of her marital status.

"Here we go!" announced Justin, handing me a glass with a rose-colored liquid, a slice of lime and a cherry visible in its clarity. "This is a kind of sangria. Dortha and I learned to love it while we were in Spain. Fruit juices, red wine, and—well, try it and see for yourself!" He turned again to Bianca. "Sure you won't join us, Bianca?"

"No, thank you, Justin," she replied coolly.

Justin held up his own glass with a flourish and said, "I think we should have some sort of toast, don't you, darling?" he asked Dortha. "Perhaps Miss Forrest or—Cameron—if I may call you by your first name?"

"Of course, although most people call me Cam."

"Then, to the successful accomplishment of a portrait of my beautiful wife that will as nearly as possible capture her true beauty."

"Oh, Justin, really—" murmured Dortha, looking embarrassed by Justin's extravagance.

"With such a subject, how could I fail?" I added smiling.

Dortha blushed, but Justin looked pleased. We all raised our glasses. I took a sip and found the drink deliciously different. A moment's silence followed Justin's elaborate toast. His eyes were on Dortha, who met them for a long moment, then looked away. I lowered my own eyes, feeling I had somehow intruded on an intimate interchange between them. But I couldn't help thinking that it would be strange indeed if Bianca did not feel uncomfortable in this halcyon atmosphere. Then I remembered that Justin's children were also here. How did they fit into what was clearly a world meant for these two newlyweds? It was difficult to imagine Dortha in the role of a stepmother to two nearly grown youngsters. She had a kind of ageless beauty, but looked barely twenty herself.

Suddenly I became aware of a lull in the conversation flowing around me. An uneasiness had entered that I could sense but not pinpoint. A tangible strain had placed an artificial quality to the words being exchanged among the other three. Every so often Justin glanced at the domed Austrian clock on the mantelpiece and shifted slightly in his chair, as if to get a better view out into the hall. I felt myself tense.

Dortha, too, seemed to be conscious of Justin's increasing nervousness, for she placed a hand on his arm once, and he patted it absentmindedly, then resolutely seemed to bring his attention back to the present. He faced me and asked intently, "Tell us how one goes about painting a portrait. I've admired the finished product, but I've often wondered how the creative process actually happens. Will you do some studies and then we'll decide on the pose or what?"

"I usually like to make some preliminary sketches, and I try to find a pose that seems most natural and comfortable to the person I'm painting. If one has never modeled, it can be quite tiring unless you're physically at ease. I like to see several possible outfits unless my subject has one special dress she wants to be painted in."

"What about that red satin off-the-shoulder evening gown we got for you in Paris?" Justin interrupted me to ask Dortha.

"Oh, Justin, that's not really *me!*" objected Dortha. "Remember, I didn't want that dress. You and the saleslady—"

"The *directoire,* my darling," corrected Justin as if admonishing a small child. "In a salon like Coudreau, one *never* says saleslady."

Dortha's cheeks flushed. "I'm sorry, I meant—"

I thought I heard a derisive little laugh from Bianca, but when I glanced at her, she was merely clearing her throat, her smooth face expressionless.

Justin covered Dortha's hand with his, leaned over, and kissed her lightly. "Never mind, sweet, I was only teasing! I'm wrong anyhow. In these days of women's lib I should say sales*person,* right? At any rate, what you wear for your portrait should really be left up to the artist, shouldn't it? After all, she has the eye for the most flattering color, what would complement the skin tones, your eyes, and hair. Am I right, Cam?"

"Usually we can come to an agreement after trying several things," I answered, not wanting to get in the middle of what might become a heated discussion. "As I said, I like to get acquainted with my subject before I really get started painting. That way I learn her taste and her preferences and we work it all out together."

Whatever might have been said next was abruptly interrupted by a great barking and the two big Weimaraners, whom I hadn't noticed sleeping under the grand piano, rushed out and slid toward the hall. There was the slam of a heavy door that reverberated through the house. Justin jumped to his feet and Dortha tipped over her glass at the startling noise. Bianca seemed the only one unmoved by all the confusion. I turned to see what it was all about and, over the sound of the dogs barking, heard a voice shout, "Shut up, damn you! Down, Bruno, down, Clovis!"

A moment later a tall boy with shaggy, shoulder-length hair, barefooted and in blue jeans, appeared in the arch of the living room door. He was followed by a slender girl similarly dressed, whose face was almost hidden by the streams of amber hair that fell from a center part to her waist. She stood with a hand on the larger dog's head, beside her brother, who stared at us belligerently.

"Aaron! Olivia! What the hell is all the racket for?" Justin demanded in an outraged voice. His face was red with anger. "Where the devil have you been? I thought you understood I wanted you dressed in suitable clothes and down here to meet our guest and ready for dinner! Instead you look like—like—" Words seemed to fail him, and he flung out his hands in a helpless gesture.

Bianca got up and moved quickly across the room to where the threesome stood glaring at each other.

"I'll handle this, Justin." She passed him and spoke in an inaudible tone to the two youngsters. Whatever she said must have been decisive enough, for they turned and walked with her out of sight down the hall—but not before the girl had tossed her hair in an arrogant way and both of them had given Justin a long, insolent stare.

A painful silence followed their departure. Justin stood uncertainly for a minute, his hands clenching and unclenching furiously. Then he came back to the fireplace and turned toward Dortha as if to say something. Instead, he sank down on one of the wing chairs that flanked the coffee table and put his head in his hands, a picture of total dejection. Dortha rose immediately from her place and knelt down beside him in a spontaneous effort to comfort him. They both seemed oblivious of my presence.

"Justin, dear, don't," Dortha said soothingly.

He shook his head as if to clear it, then took his hands away from his face and said in a harsh voice, "I think they do it on purpose to upset me." He seemed to remember me, for he looked at me apologetically and said, "How can I excuse my children's rudeness? It's *in*excusable. But I can apologize for my own behavior. I'm ashamed to have exposed you to a family scene. The truth of it is I've been away from my children for a considerable amount of time. I don't know how to treat them or how to control them anymore. Bianca is good with them, though. She seems to understand young people better than I. All I can say is that I'm very sorry, and I hope we can salvage something of this evening."

Somehow I managed to comment on a particularly lovely urn on the mantel and, while Justin gradually recovered himself, Dortha gratefully told me of the day they had discovered it in a small, out-of-the-way shop in southern France. The awkward scene was not mentioned again, but it lingered in all our minds. Eventually Bianca returned and reseated herself without explanation. Within a few minutes Rachel came to the door and announced dinner.

The dining room could have been a reproduction of a medieval baronial hall. Heavy wood beams formed a cathedral arch; rough plaster walls were hung with Spanish paintings, authentic shields, and arms. A long banquet table of massive oak reinforced the effect and in the center were two seven-branched Russian candlesticks with burning candles.

The four of us took our places, but the two other high-backed carved chairs were conspicuously vacant. No one said anything about the missing youngsters and, as Rachel and another younger woman began to serve, I assumed we were going to eat without Aaron and Olivia.

The meal was gourmet—a rack of lamb, fresh vegetables, and avocado salad with two kinds of wines served with each course; dessert was a brandied fruit compote.

Conversation centered mainly on the Bradfords' European stay, with Justin holding forth on nearly every aspect of their trip. Dortha merely nodded or murmured assent when Justin asked her to clarify a date or the exact place, but otherwise she remained silent. Bianca said very little, but I noticed that she gave silent serving directions to the help. It was she who rose first and suggested, "Shall we have our coffee and liqueur in the living room?"

It was easy to see that Bianca was in charge of this household.

Justin had gained control of his emotions over the unpleasant scene earlier and, as we sat drinking demitasse from tiny, gold-rimmed porcelain cups, he asked me, "Now, where would you like to work, Cam? I suppose lighting is important. Where would a good north light be in this house, do you think, Bianca?"

She gave an indifferent shrug, so I spoke directly to Justin. "The light is important, but of course we can always augment natural light with a well-placed spotlight or other arrangement. As a matter of fact, the light in my guest cottage with that large window might be just right. That way I could continue working even after the time of Mrs. Bradford's sitting." I turned to Dortha. "Perhaps it would be a good idea if you came down tomorrow, and we could experiment with poses and lighting."

Dortha seemed to be lost in her own thoughts and did not reply. Justin raised his voice sharply to her.

"Dortha, dear, Miss Forrest suggests you go to her cottage tomorrow so she can do some preliminary work for your portrait."

Dortha started and said vaguely, "Oh, yes, I suppose that would be all right. Anything you and Miss Forrest decide." Her voice trailed off wearily, and she passed a slender hand across her forehead. Justin was immediately all concern.

"Is something the matter, darling? Aren't you feeling well?" he asked solicitously.

"Nothing serious, just a slight headache coming on," she replied, darting an anxious look in Bianca's direction.

I followed the look and saw a rather contemptuous expression pass over Bianca's smooth face.

"Maybe you should go upstairs then, dear," Justin said gently. To all of us he said, "Perhaps it would be wise for us to call it an evening. It's been a long day and a tiring trip for Cam as well. I spent several hours at my desk, unproductive as they were, and goodness knows Bianca never stops from morning till night. Dortha, you took a longer than usual walk this afternoon, didn't you, dear? You were gone over two hours, I believe."

Dortha reddened under her translucent skin, her hands twisted in her lap. She seemed disconcerted by Justin's remark, or was I seeing too much in this room with these people? I chided myself. I'd have to be careful, keep a firm check on my imagination or whatever it was that always seemed to see beneath the surface of things and individuals.

"I'll just walk our guest to her cottage," Justin continued. "You and she can work out the details on the sketching session tomorrow. What time would you like Dortha to come, Cam?"

"Whatever time suits you, Mrs. Bradford," I said. I felt somewhat uncomfortable by Dortha's lack of participation in the arrangements for her own portrait. "Would eleven be okay?"

"Yes, that will be fine." Dortha got to her feet. She seemed agitated as she moved to the door. Then a petulant voice stopped her.

"Aunt Bianca, is there anything left to eat?"

Looking in the direction from which the voice had come, I saw Olivia Bradford in a man's denim work shirt, her long, slender legs bare and her head wrapped turban fashion in a towel. The impatient tone and the bored expression was, I felt, for the express purpose of infuriating her father.

Bianca answered calmly, "Rachel has something on the sideboard on warmers in the pantry. Where is Aaron?"

"Beats me!" retorted the girl, turning away without a backward glance or a word to anyone. She sauntered down the hall and out of sight.

There was a moment's silence, then Justin spoke quietly to Dortha. "You go along, darling. I'll be up after I take Miss Forrest to her cottage."

CHAPTER 5

Outside, the fog had dropped, wrapping the tops of the pine trees in a gauzy veil, shrouding all but a few steps in front of us as Justin and I made our way down the path. It was slow going, but at last we reached my doll's house in the woods.

As I stepped inside, I saw that a new fire had been laid and lamps were turned on, another example of Bianca's expert hostessing, I thought.

Justin seemed to hesitate a little before going. He cleared his throat a little nervously then said, "I hope you won't judge us by my offsprings' performance tonight. We're still on a shakedown cruise as a family. For the last four years they've been at boarding school and Bianca has been looking after them during vacations—since their mother died. I've been wandering around the world gathering material. I've seen them only at brief intervals—here in the summers, in Switzerland on their school holidays. They're not used to me as an authority in their lives. Then Dortha is only eight years older than Aaron, so he can hardly accept her as his stepmother." Justin paused. There was an air of tension about him that made me uneasy. His desperate urgency to have Dortha's portrait painted seemed unnatural.

My unspoken question must have transmitted itself to Justin, for in the next moment he tried to explain. "I'm sure you're familiar with Keats's poem, 'Ode on a Grecian Urn,' aren't you?" he said. "Maybe that's what I'm trying to do with Dortha—immortalize her at the time of her greatest beauty, capture the moment of happiness—" He quoted, " 'She cannot fade . . . For ever wilt thou love, and she be fair!' " Justin gave a self-conscious laugh. "You see, Miss Forrest, I'm not just a hack writer who turns out popular novels. I'm a romantic."

He turned to leave, but before he opened the cottage door, he said, "I want your stay here to be pleasant, for the painting of the portrait to go well. If there are problems with the kids and Dortha's upset—" He hesitated.

I knew he wanted some kind of reassurance from me, and although there was no way that I could promise the sittings and outcome would be successful, I said, "Oh, I think things will work out. Sometimes it takes a person a while to relax when they're having a portrait done. But I noticed there's a stereo here, and we can play tapes of music Dortha likes to listen to. She may even enjoy the experience."

Still Justin frowned.

I did not know what else I could say to convince him. In fact, his doubts were beginning to affect me. Then Justin flashed a big smile and said heartily, "Forgive me, Miss Forrest. It's probably just me. When I'm having difficulty with my own creative work, I'm apt to borrow trouble. You're right. Everything is going to be just fine. Good night now. Sleep well."

But I didn't.

After Justin left, I put a match to the newly laid fire, poured myself a small glass of cream sherry from a cut-glass decanter, and curled up among the cushions on the sofa. I had hoped to unwind a bit from my stimulating day of new experiences, but troubling thoughts kept surfacing —thoughts that later penetrated into my dreams.

The painfully tense situation that existed at Gull's Glen was undeniable. Would I become caught up in the tangled relationships, and would my work suffer as a result?

These questions were still unanswered when I went to bed. In spite of the drink, the warmth of the fire in the corner fireplace of the bedroom, the luxurious softness of the scented sheets, the satin quilt, and the comfortable bed, I tossed and turned. Random, confused thoughts collided as I grew sleepier. The closed, sullen faces of Justin's children floated in and out of my consciousness, along with Dortha's frightened look.

Sometime during the night I was awakened by the sound of heavy rain. Evidently the storm that had threatened all afternoon had broken, and it was pouring. I snuggled deeper into the covers and went back to sleep.

When I next opened my eyes, the cold, gray light of dawn had seeped into the room. I sat up in bed shivering. The fire had gone out and at first I felt disoriented, not remembering immediately where I was. Then I heard the persistent clicking noise that must have awakened me. I saw that one of the casement windows had blown open. I reached for my robe, dragged it on, and slipped out of bed.

Outside, a misty wind was tossing the branches of the surrounding Monterey pines in a weird dance. Low fog clung to the ground, rising like smoky shreds of cotton.

I was pulling in the window to latch it when I saw something that caught my attention. At first I thought it must be a tree bough blown down by the wind. Then, as I leaned forward to get a better look, I gasped and drew back. A ghostlike figure seemed to approach the cottage. Shrouded in a capelike garment, it moved swiftly along the path through the woods. As I stood watching, it disappeared into a veil of drifting fog. I blinked, not knowing whether it was a trick of mist and rain that had caused some sort of optical illusion, or if what I'd seen had been real.

Just as I decided it must be my imagination, I saw the two Bradford dogs loping along the path as though they were following that person—or thing—I'd seen.

Hurriedly I banged the window shut, and scuttled back to my warm bed.

I lay there for a few minutes more trying to get back to sleep. Finally I gave up, got out of bed, and went out to the front room. I got some logs from the wood basket beside the fireplace and some kindling and with the help of some crumpled newspapers got a fire going. The vigorous activity warmed me up considerably. Then I went in search of the makings for coffee. By the time I was sipping on my first cup, the apparition I'd seen earlier seemed less frightening.

Most likely it was someone from the main house out jogging in a hooded sweater of some kind. Probably Justin. He might be a health nut, into diet and exercise to keep his trim, youthful physique. By the time I had my second cup I had dismissed the eerie incident as unimportant.

I started thinking about Dortha's portrait and the first sitting that would take place that day.

I began to feel an anticipatory excitement that had been lacking in me all spring when I had simply plodded through my classes trying to forget Doug. Now I had that stirring of creativity, that precious urge to paint that I had temporarily lost.

I couldn't wait for Dortha to come so we could get started. I hoped she would overcome her reluctance to have her portrait painted, and I wondered again what had happened since that day at Aunt Mim's when she had seemed to share Justin's enthusiasm about it.

A portrait is a joint venture between the sitter and the artist. Its success or failure depends on both. It is different from painting a still life when only the artist needs to satisfy himself. In a portrait whatever is happening to the model, inside or even in a pose he finds difficult to maintain, can alter the mood necessary for an artist to do his best work.

That's why I wanted to make sure everything was just right for Dortha. I could not forget some of the things I'd observed about her the night before. Even though there was nothing I could do about the unhappy atmosphere in that house, I could try to create a climate of pleasant warmth here at the cottage so that Dortha would relax during her sittings.

I decided to make some preparations. I looked around to see where I would place my easel, and set up my painting box and other equipment.

I wanted to get my drawing pencils sharpened and decide which size of the new sketchbooks I'd bought in Carmel I wanted to use for my preliminary sketches.

To my dismay, after looking all over the cottage, I could not find the package of art materials I'd purchased at Jeff Maxwell's store. Had I left it in the car? I'd check when I went up to the house for breakfast. It was now after nine o'clock, although the heavy fog made it seem much earlier. Surely everyone was up by now.

I put on slacks and a warm sweater, tied a scarf around my head, and started out. Fog was dripping off the trees but even so there was a kind of glare that indicated the sun was trying to burn through it. I took the path along the seawall instead of the one through the woods, as it seemed to be clearing more that way. I could hear the surf booming below and felt the salt spray in my face. I walked carefully, remembering Justin's warning last night about the slickness of the rocks. The fog blown by the sea wind parted like a transparent curtain as I walked forward.

Suddenly I became aware of voices. I stopped, listening, wondering if it had just been the pounding of the waves reverberating as they crashed against the rocks. I could see nothing because of the dense fog, but the voices became louder, as if raised in loud argument, and I knew they were human—a man's and a woman's.

I stood still, frozen in an agony of indecision. I could not tell where they were coming from, ahead or behind me, so I didn't know whether to turn back or go forward. I did not want to stumble into a private spat between my employers. For by this time, although I'd never heard it at that pitch, I was positive that the woman's voice was Dortha Bradford's.

"It wasn't my idea to come back here at all! Now I know it was a mistake! How can you do this to me? How can you be so cruel?"

The man's voice seemed to cut her off, but it was impossible to hear his words, they were so muffled in the fog.

My heart was pounding. I certainly did not want to get into the middle of this. Not waiting to hear anything else, I turned and practically ran back to the guest cottage. I let myself in, shed my jacket, and breathing rapidly flung myself down on one of the chairs.

My mind couldn't make any sense out of the exchange I'd overheard. Obviously it was not intended for a third party. No matter what they were quarreling about, there was a frightening element in it. Whatever it was, it was no petty disagreement.

I was at least thankful I'd avoided the double embarrassment of coming upon them out of the fog with no warning. I winced at the thought of such an encounter. Even now I cringed at the knowledge that I'd still have to face Dortha and Justin after inadvertently overhearing them quarrel.

I felt like packing up and taking off. The dream job was turning into a nightmare. There were so many complicated relationships and undercurrents at Gull's Glen, I wondered if a good sitting was possible. I poured myself another cup of coffee and worried. Finally I decided I'd have to stay and paint the portrait, muddling through the best I could and trying not to get involved in the personal problems of the people at Gull's Glen.

I waited for what I felt was an adequate length of time,

then started out again. The fog was blowing away now, and I could see a stretch of beach and the gray, angry-looking sea. Below was a crescent-shaped cove, and I stopped for a moment to look at the view.

That was when I saw two figures in the distance just emerging from the rocky cliffs onto the sand, then head up the beach in the opposite direction. One of them was wearing a flowing hooded cape. Dortha and Justin? I wondered. I hoped they had made up after their quarrel.

I continued toward the house and even before I saw its outline in the mist, I heard the dogs barking. As I approached, the two Weimaraners came leaping out of the fog like the gray ghosts in those old English mystery movies. I stood still as they circled me, sniffing and making small whining noises. Evidently they recognized me and came closer, their heavy tails whipping my legs. I rubbed their noses, patted them for a little while, then with them as escorts went on up the terrace steps to the front door. While I hesitated there, not knowing whether to ring the doorbell or just walk in, my decision was made for me. The door was flung open and there, in a terrycloth monk's robe, stood Justin.

I was stunned speechless at first, as I realized with a sinking sensation that the man with whom Dortha had argued so violently, and later walked with along the ocean's edge, was not Justin.

CHAPTER 6

"Good morning, Miss Forrest," he greeted me heartily. "Come in. I trust you slept well?" he asked, not waiting for my answer. "I can't say the same for myself. I was too keyed-up to sleep after I got back up to the house last night. I worked most of the night, to tell you the truth. I think I've licked my writer's block. Thought I'd just jot down a few ideas and by golly, I got going and it was dawn before I knew it. It happens sometimes like that. I've just showered and was having my coffee."

Justin led the way into the dining room where a sumptuous breakfast buffet was set out on the massive sideboard. There were scrambled eggs and sausages in an ornate silver chafing dish, racks of toast, an assortment of sweet rolls, slices of fresh cantaloupe.

"Now eat heartily, Miss Forrest," he urged. "Be sure to take enough. We're all on our own for lunch, you know. I don't eat lunch myself. Solitary, sedentary work like mine tends to put weight on a person unless you're careful. I try to get regular exercise—usually a walk on the beach, after I do my daily stint at the typewriter."

Although I wasn't used to eating such a big breakfast, with Justin hovering I helped myself to the eggs and toast, and a slice of fruit. As I seated myself at the table, Justin poured me a cup of coffee from the large silver urn. He refilled his own cup and sat down opposite me.

"Am I the only late arrival?" I asked.

"Not at all. The children sleep until noon and straggle down at all hours. But Bianca is up with the birds and busy about—" he shrugged and smiled "—her managing. I'm usually up and at my desk by eight, but as I mentioned, this morning was an exception. As for Dortha, she had a headache last night and is sleeping late. As a matter of fact, I insisted she take a sedative and I thought I'd just let her sleep until she wakes up."

I gave him a quick look. Dortha sleeping late? Then it could not have been Dortha I heard arguing with someone in the fog! Could I have been mistaken? I'd been so sure I recognized her distinctively husky voice.

"She wasn't feeling at all well," Justin continued, "and

I do want her to be fresh for her sitting. I hope you don't mind postponing it, perhaps, for today, Miss Forrest?"

"Not at all. I'm sorry Mrs. Bradford isn't feeling well, but I can certainly find things to do. I think I'd like to explore the beach . . . that is when the fog lifts."

"A great idea!" Justin said enthusiastically. "Actually, I was going to suggest that very thing. There's a secluded cove just below our property, a nice stretch of beach to walk. Interesting, too, tide pools, and all kinds of shells and rocks, if you're interested in that sort of thing." He paused. "I am. I love this area. This coastline is more beautiful than anything in Europe . . . Costa del Sol, the Riviera . . . nothing compares to this stark, rocky part of California."

At that moment we were interrupted by Bianca's voice from the doorway.

"Justin, the maids want to know—" She halted as she saw me, gave me a brief nod, and an abrupt, "Good morning, Miss Forrest," then continued speaking to Justin in an annoyed tone.

"The sofa-bed in your study—do you want it remade? Rachel and Agnes were almost through downstairs when they noticed it had been slept in last night."

Justin reddened under his tan.

"Oh, yes, Bianca, by all means, have them take off the sheets and blanket. It's not necessary for them to remake it. I won't be sleeping there again tonight. Dortha had a beastly headache and took some sleeping pills, and I did some work on my book until quite late last night, and I didn't want to disturb her."

"Very well," was all she said in reply, but I sensed an implied note of skepticism that I thought quite rude. It was becoming more and more clear to me that their relationship was even stranger than it seemed. Why did Justin put up with her barely suppressed antagonism? I had no time to give it any thought, for she addressed me next.

"You did understand about lunch, didn't you, Miss Forrest?"

"Oh, yes, thank you. Breakfast is delicious. I usually don't eat this much. It will certainly hold me until dinner," I said.

"Perhaps you will want to keep something more in the small fridge at the cottage," said Bianca, "so that when you and Dortha are working you can fix something for the two of you at lunchtime?"

"That's a wonderful idea!" Justin exclaimed. "A great suggestion, Bianca. If Miss Forrest is like most creative people, when their work is going well they hate to stop . . . even to eat. Cheese, fruit, coffee—something light is usually enough for me when I'm working. But I don't want Dortha to get overtired, and I notice when she doesn't eat properly she gets very weak."

I caught a glimpse of Bianca's expression as Justin had turned toward me, and I was shocked by its open look of disgust. Evidently she did not sympathize with the new Mrs. Bradford's tendency to faintness. But then, after all, her sister had once been Justin's bride. Maybe he had not been as solicitous of her health. What was behind that look she had just cast upon Justin?

As I left the house and started down the path in the direction Justin told me would lead to the beach, I scolded myself.

You've got to stop analyzing everything and everyone here. You're here to paint Dortha Bradford's portrait, that's all, not try to figure out the complicated relationships at Gull's Glen, I reminded myself sternly.

As the fog rolled upward, a pale sun broke through and it promised to be a glorious day.

I kept looking for a break in the seawall to climb over so I could get down to the beach, but instead I saw two wooden posts that indicated steps. When I reached them,

I almost changed my mind about trying to get down to the cove.

There was a sheer drop onto the rocks, and as I looked down, I automatically backed away from the edge, feeling slightly dizzy. After a moment I moved to the top step, and holding on with both hands to either side, I beheld a breathtaking view. I could see in both directions the rugged line of the coast and the ocean. Below, the ocean surged and flung itself against the jutting rocks.

Even though the steps appeared almost as treacherous to navigate as the cliffs, the crescent beach below, its smooth sand washed clean by the tide and the dark blue ocean, looked too inviting to resist.

When I'd finally maneuvered the hazardous steps down to the beach, I took off my shoes and walked barefoot along the edge of the ocean, letting the fans of foamy sea water wash over my feet.

Driftwood littered the sand, its twisted natural sculpture adding unique beauty to the isolated beach. Rocks of different sizes, some gleaming underwater like rare jade, tempted until my pockets hung heavy with them. In the tide pools sea life thrived. There were shells of endless fascination—sand dollars, abandoned mussel shells, angel wings, and a few that must have been washed in from some faraway place.

The fog was still rising along the sand and melting away like shreds of gray cotton. Just as I was relishing the solitude of having the whole beach to myself, I saw the figure of a man walking toward me.

As he came closer, I observed that he was tall and leanly built. He was wearing a dark blue Windbreaker and khaki pants. His hair was the color of sand with sun-bleached streaks. As we came nearly parallel, he lifted his hand in a sort of salute, but didn't speak. I noticed he had straight, even features, but since he was wearing dark glasses, I could not see his eyes and it gave him a curiously blank look.

After he had passed, I had a strange, reaction, the kind of uneasy feeling you get when you've thought you were alone, then discovered someone has been watching you. It was an unpleasant sensation, and I tried to shake it off as I continued my walk.

It was probably the dark glasses, I told myself, thinking about the man. Eyes were so important to a face. I knew that in painting a portrait the face did not really come alive until you painted the eyes—and got them right.

CHAPTER 7

"Now what in the world could have happened to them?" I asked myself for the dozenth time. I had searched the little guest cottage and my car thoroughly and the package of new art supplies was definitely missing. Maybe I had left them at the shop or at the restaurant where I ate lunch in Carmel.

The only thing to do was to retrace my steps, I decided. If no one had turned in my lost package, I would just have to buy more supplies.

As I headed toward Carmel that afternoon, I thought the trip was not entirely an unpleasant chore. It might be nice to see that attractive young man, Jeff Maxwell, again.

The minute I walked in the door of the store, he looked up and a big grin broke across his tan face.

"Well, Miss Forrest, you sure go through supplies in record time. Or did you forget something?" He got up and came around the counter. "Whatever, I'm glad you came back. I was sorry I was tied up with that other customer, I wanted to speak to you before you left yesterday."

Well, at least he remembered me, I thought with a small lift of my spirits.

"As a matter of fact, I somehow managed to misplace or lose all the things I bought here," I explained.

"Unless I left my package here?" I added hopefully.

Jeff shook his head. "I'm sorry, no."

"Well, I may have left it where I ate lunch. Only I can't remember exactly where the little restaurant was," I said sheepishly. "There are so many and I just kind of wandered around yesterday, not really paying too much attention to the streets. A typical tourist, I guess." I laughed finally.

"That's really too bad." Jeff frowned. "Of course, we can fix you up again here with everything you need, but it doesn't make up for what you've lost. I'll tell you what, if you haven't had lunch yet, let me take you. In a way that may compensate."

I hesitated, but only for a minute. Jeff was certainly attractive and friendly.

"Thanks, I'd like to," I answered.

"Just give me a minute to put a sign on the door, and we're off," he said.

"It's such a nice day, let's see if we can get a table outdoors at The Harbinger," Jeff suggested as we started down the cobblestone street after leaving the shop.

A few minutes later we were seated in the pleasant sunshine near the fountain at the center of Carmel Plaza. We were surrounded by a whole complex of stores and shops I had not seen before, three tiers of them, each with its deck bordered with flower boxes of blooming, cascading flowers.

"Carmel is really like being in another world. Everything is so charming and pretty it's almost unreal," I told Jeff.

He nodded. "I know what you mean. I felt like that myself the first few weeks I lived here. I felt I would wake up soon and discover I'd dreamed it all." He shook his head. You know, "I came down here on a weekend, saw the framing shop was for sale, and practically bought it sight unseen. When I got back to San Francisco that Monday, I thought I must have been temporarily insane. You see, I was a junior partner in a Montgomery Street brokerage firm, the typical rising young executive and this was a total departure." He laughed. "The people I knew there—some of them, anyway—thought I'd lost my mind when I told them what I'd done. Others said they envied me. I've never regretted my decision for a single moment. In fact, sometimes I wonder why I didn't do it sooner." He stopped and raised one eyebrow quizzically in a way I was beginning to recognize as characteristic, and demanded, "Do you know any other thirty-year-old dropouts?"

I smiled. "I can't say that I blame you. It wouldn't be hard to get spoiled by a place like this."

Just then the waiter brought our quiche and salad. I realized I was hungrier than I'd thought.

"It's not a matter of getting spoiled. I mean, the lifestyle here, it's not just for the very, very rich, if that's what you think," Jeff continued as we ate.

"After all, I figure you have to earn a living, you have to have a place to live, food, some intellectual stimulation, some recreation—why not find all those things in the most pleasant place possible?"

I held up both hands in a helpless gesture. "I give up! Where else but Carmel?"

"Right!" he conceded, laughing. "I hope I haven't bored you. I begin to sound like a walking Chamber of Commerce."

"Not at all! I find it very refreshing to meet someone who is so content."

"Well, not completely. There are some things missing in my life right now, but I'll tell you about that some other time," he said with a teasing grin. "I hope there will be a next time?"

"More coffee?" the waiter interrupted, and Jeff's question went unanswered.

We finished lunch and walked back to the store.

While we began to collect the supplies to replace the ones that had disappeared, I asked Jeff to tell me what he had started to about the tragedy that had taken place at Gull's Glen.

I felt I knew him a little better now, and knowing what had happened might give me some insight on the odd situation I was now aware existed there.

"How about some coffee while I tell you what I know about it?" he suggested.

We went back into the main part of the store. From a blue enameled pot Jeff poured me a mug of hot, fragrant coffee. I waved away his offer of cream and sugar, and we settled down on two cane-seated stools.

"Rosalind Bradford, Justin's first wife, was an actress," Jeff explained. "As I understand it, she was on her way to becoming nationally known when they married. In any case, she was well known around here for her activities in local theater. She was different-looking, very vivacious, friendly, and well liked by everyone. That's why it was such a shock when—" He stopped, then frowned.

"Rosalind was found on the cliffs just below Gull's Glen—her neck was broken. She was dead when they found her. She had fallen . . . or slipped in the dark." He hesitated a long time, then reluctantly finished. "You see there was some question about her death . . . whether it was accidental or—"

"Or?"

"The subject of suicide was brought up, but that was ruled out by most everyone that had known her. Then, there were some wild rumors. Finally there was an accusation that it had been, perhaps, murder."

"Murder!" I gasped.

"That instead of falling she may have been pushed or thrown. But in the end the coroner's jury gave a verdict of accidental death. You see, she was—coincidentally—having *her* portrait painted at the time. A young fellow, whom I knew because, of course, he came in here often and everyone knew he'd been commissioned to do her portrait. His name was Cole Burnham, a very promising artist. It was obvious to everyone that he was terribly distraught over her death. He was the one who made the accusations."

"Against whom?"

Jeff looked down into his coffee mug. "I wish I hadn't said anything about any of this—" he said haltingly.

"Well, please," I protested. "Whom did he accuse?"

"Justin. Justin Bradford."

I drew in my breath sharply. "No!"

Jeff shook his head. "It was a bad time. In a small community like this, where the people who live here year-round form a close circle, it shocked everyone. It was Bianca—Bianca Matthews, Rosalind's sister—who took the witness stand in Justin's defense. She was very eloquent about Justin's devotion to Rosalind and testified that his having anything to do with her death was unthinkable."

The bell over the door jangled. Jeff put down his coffee cup and went to the counter.

I sat there letting my coffee get cold, stunned by what I had just learned.

"Why, hello, Ennis, when did you get back?" As Jeff's voice raised in greeting, a man's image projected itself into my numbed consciousness.

"A few days ago. I've got an exhibit coming up in San Francisco in the next couple of weeks, and I've brought in some of my photographs to be framed."

Casually I turned to look at the newcomer, who was laying out a large portfolio on the wide top surface of the counter. At the same time he turned an indifferent gaze on me.

In a flash of delayed recognition, I saw it was the same

man I'd passed on the beach. But then he had on dark glasses and I hadn't seen his eyes. Now I saw he had that kind of brooding good looks sometimes considered to be romantic, as though he were harboring some secret sorrow. His eyes were a curious shade of gray-green, like the ocean before a storm. . . .

He showed no reciprocal recognition as Jeff introduced us. "Miss Cameron Forrest, this is Ennis Shelby. Miss Forrest is here to paint a portrait of Justin Bradford's new wife."

Here there was an immediate reaction. Something curious flickered in Ennis Shelby's eyes as they lingered on me speculatively.

"Justin has a real penchant for immortalizing his wives on canvas, wouldn't you say, Jeff?" he said indolently. A slow smile tugged at his sensuous mouth as he gave a sort of mock bow toward me. "No offense meant, Miss Forrest. It's just that there was a rather unfortunate connection with portrait painting at Gull's Glen not too long ago. It has nothing to do with you, of course. I wish you the best of luck with yours." His face remained impassive. Then, with a nod almost of dismissal to me, he turned back and began discussing his photographs with Jeff.

I felt a little awkward but decided to stay and finish my coffee, hoping to get a little more information from Jeff before I left.

Their conversation was highly technical, pertaining to specifications of the framing of Ennis's photographs. Decisions of sizes, colors of mats, the ultimate type of frame, were discussed at length. Finally concluded, a time for delivery arrived at, Ennis Shelby turned to leave. His eyes rested on me for a long moment, then a genuine smile appeared on his face, making me aware again of how handsome he was.

"Well, good-bye, Miss Forrest. I'm really glad to have met you. Forgive me for seeming preoccupied just now. I have an important show coming up. But I do hope to see you again while you're in Carmel. We're neighbors of sorts, you know. I have a beach shack just off the cliffs below Gull's Glen."

With the same odd little salute he'd given me on the beach that morning, Ennis Shelby went out of the shop.

I glanced at Jeff, who shrugged.

"Odd sort of guy, but an excellent photographer. His work has won all kinds of awards. I feel flattered that he brings his prints to me to be framed. I mean, he could have them done in San Francisco."

"I had an instructor once who told me framing was an art equally as important as painting. So you must be good enough to warrant his trust," I replied.

"Thanks, I needed that," he quipped.

As I got up to leave, Jeff said, "I hope my telling you about the trouble at Gull's Glen hasn't spoiled things for you—the work, the portrait—put a pall on things there for you."

"No, don't worry about it. It's all in the past and I'm sure it won't affect my work on this portrait. I'm looking forward to painting Dortha Bradford. She's very beautiful."

"Aren't they the hardest ones to paint? Some old grizzled fisherman with lots of character could be easier. I've heard it's the relatives that give a portrait artist the most trouble." He took a stance as though viewing a painting, squinted his eyes, and shook his head. Putting on a querulous voice, he said, "No, that's not Uncle Harry's chin, is it, Mabel? There's something about the eyes that are just not right!"

I laughed. "That's very good! But I don't think I'll have exactly that problem. Pleasing Justin is the main thing I'm concerned about. He's very much in love with his wife and—well, the portrait has to look the way he sees her."

"You'll do a fine job, I'm sure."

"You say that without ever having seen any of my paintings?" I asked him in mock surprise.

"Bring some in, why don't you. I'm always looking for new artists for the gallery."

"I haven't anything with me, but I do hope to do a lot of painting this summer after I finish Dortha's portrait." I started toward the door. "Well, thanks for all your help."

"Will you be in again—soon?" he asked.

I looked down at my big bundle and said, "Well, probably not *soon*. I think I've got quite enough to see me through this portrait." I was surprised and pleased to notice that Jeff seemed disappointed, so I added, "But I'll be back to your gallery. You've got some very interesting work I'd like to take more time studying."

"Good. I'll look forward to that." He grinned.

Back in my car heading for Gull's Glen, I decided I liked Jeff Maxwell. He was intelligent and sensitive and had a low-key but keen sense of humor, besides being an artist in his own right. Nice looking, too, if I were interested—which I most certainly wasn't.

My mind turned to Ennis Shelby. What a strange, enigmatic person he seemed to be. I vaguely recognized the name. I must have once read a review of one of his exhibits in the San Francisco papers.

All in all, it had been an interesting afternoon. In a way I wished I hadn't learned about the tragic death of Rosalind Bradford or of its aftermath. Poor Justin! No wonder he had an obsession with having Dortha painted at this time in their marriage. What was it he had said to me—"before anything happens to spoil it"? He seemed to have an almost superstitious belief or premonition about the transitory nature of things. It made his protective affection for her more understandable. Losing his first wife like that would make any man doubly anxious to hold on to his second chance at happiness.

It also explained somewhat Bianca Matthews's position at Gull's Glen. Justin owed her a debt of gratitude. From what Jeff had said, her testimony probably saved him from being indicted for his wife's murder.

Even though I'd told Jeff it wouldn't, this information had altered my attitude. In spite of everything, it had placed a kind of oppressive sadness on the whole situation.

As I turned off the highway and onto the private road, I told myself firmly that what I needed to do was to get to work. I just hoped Dortha would be ready to start the sittings tomorrow.

CHAPTER 8

When I went up to the house for dinner that evening, I wished again that Jeff Maxwell had never told me about Rosalind Bradford's death and the tragic aftermath. It made me look at everyone at Gull's Glen with an entirely different perspective.

The youngsters, Aaron and Olivia, were late coming to the table, which brought a scowl to Justin's face. I saw Dortha tense immediately, as though bracing herself for another confrontation. Only Bianca seemed unaffected by their tardy arrival, or at least she did not evidence any displeasure. Service of the soup course began and almost at once the sounds of slurping were louder than the conversation that Justin was striving to initiate. I could see him visibly struggle to control his impulse to turn toward Aaron and demand him to stop. I risked a glance at the boy and thought, *He's deliberately antagonizing his father.*

Aaron's handsome young face was half hidden by the shock of unkempt curls, his arms rested on the table, and his head was bent over the soup bowl a short distance from the rim as he spooned the liquid sloppily into his mouth.

The noise gradually became so obvious, it was impossible to ignore it. Even anticipating the explosion, I was startled when it came.

Justin's fist came down on the table so hard the crystal goblets shook.

"Damnit, Aaron, sit up and eat properly!"

His voice was angry and harsh and everyone jumped as it hammered out the command to his son.

I glanced quickly around the table at the faces staring at Justin and saw they mirrored my own shock. That is, all except Aaron, who was leveling a look so full of arrogant defiance at Justin that I felt myself shiver.

"If you can't come to dinner clean, brushed, and dressed and conduct yourself in a decent, mannerly way, by gad, don't come at all!"

Dortha was deathly pale, her wide eyes darting from Aaron to Justin, then lowering to her own place. Bianca, her chin lifted, seemed about to intervene; then, as though she thought better of it, she bit her lip and her mouth tightened into a straight line. Everyone was literally holding their breath, when I saw out of the corner of my eye an incredible gesture. Olivia's hand reached out and purposely tipped over her glass of ice water, its contents spilling out onto the polished surface of the table, the ice cubes rolling toward the center.

That was too much for Justin. He flung down his napkin and shouted, "All right, both of you! If you can't behave like civilized human beings with proper manners, then you needn't dine with the adults!"

At this point Aaron stood up, knocking over his chair as he did so and yelled back at Justin, "Who in hell wants to?" With that he rushed out of the room and Olivia ran out after him.

There was a stunned silence.

Justin, making a great effort to get himself under control, said in a strained voice, "I apologize, Miss Forrest, for subjecting you to such a scene, but my children have got to be taught better manners. It's disgraceful—"

Bianca's cool voice interrupted him.

"You're probably right, Justin. Their manners could stand improvement. However, I feel they are just acting out a certain amount of frustration. They weren't this way before you and Dortha arrived. You'll just have to give them time—"

He cut her short.

"How long do they need to behave like decent, well-mannered young adults? I'm paying thousands of dollars to send them to schools where they're supposed to produce people with some social graces."

Again Bianca's tone was icy.

"Don't you think we should discuss this later, Justin? This can hardly be of much interest to Miss Forrest."

Justin again seemed to struggle to contain his anger. Dortha looked miserable. I saw her hand go tentatively out to pat Justin's fist, which was clenched, then she drew it back.

Fortunately at this moment Rachel and the man servant brought in the food trolley from which they lifted the roast for Justin to carve; they began circling the table with the vegetable platters for us to help ourselves. Nothing was said while this was being done.

There is something to be said for people of sophistication and good background, I thought, because after the servants had departed, everyone tried to reestablish some semblance of normal conversation.

Maybe it was to be expected, but the atmosphere almost visibly relaxed once the children had left the room. Justin gradually became expansive and beamingly refilled the wine glasses, Bianca began asking me about the school where I'd taught, and Dortha seemed less acutely tense.

At last the meal was over, and after coffee and liqueur in the living room, I felt I could legitimately take my leave. Even though on the surface we four adults had managed to carry on as though the abrasive confrontation between Justin and the children had not occurred, I felt it would be tactful for me to give the three of them a chance to discuss the problem without an outsider present.

Leaving Justin and Dortha sitting side by side on the couch in front of the fire, unobtrusively holding hands, Bianca walked with me to the front hall. In a low tone of voice she brought the subject of the dinner scene up herself.

"I don't want to involve you unnecessarily in our family affairs, Miss Forrest, but I do feel you are owed some sort of explanation for Aaron and Olivia's behavior. They really are wonderful children basically. But they have come through a terrible time. A few years ago my sister died suddenly . . . and it hasn't been easy for them to accept Justin's remarriage . . . and Dortha . . ." She paused significantly. "I do think, though, that Justin is right, that they should eat alone for a while. There is no use aggravating an already raw situation. I think they'd rather, anyhow. And, of course, that way Justin can prolong his honeymoon." I detected a note of sarcasm creeping into her words. "It is rather hard for them, and I hope you can appreciate that and try to understand and not dislike them. You see, they absolutely adored Rosalind." Another long pause and Bianca's face showed traces of what must still be a painful memory for her. "But then, everyone did."

Her face hardened suddenly and she said, "Justin just has to realize that not everyone can forget so quickly or destroy the past so completely and go on as if—" She broke off abruptly.

Her eyes narrowed speculatively. I felt somehow she was taking my measure, trying to decide whether to tell me something. At length, she must have decided against it, for she moved to the door.

I did not know exactly how to reply, but I murmured

something to the effect that I taught teen-agers and knew something of their mood swings and behavior.

"Thank you. That's very gracious of you to say." Bianca gave me a fleeting smile. Then, "Have you a flashlight, and a wrap of some kind? It tends to get quite chilly here at night."

I had worn a coat sweater and assured her I was beginning to know my way back from the main house to the guest house, and so said good night.

It had been a long evening, and I didn't realize how much tension I had absorbed until I tried to go to sleep.

What had Bianca been trying to tell me, I wondered. It was almost as if she were warning me, or perhaps planting a seed of suspicion about Justin in my mind.

I got into bed, but the strange mood of the evening still hovered, plaguing my mind relentlessly. Again, the unusual mix of relationships under one roof struck me as incredibly complex and inevitably triggered conflict.

It has nothing to do with me, I tried to tell myself as I tossed and turned, restlessly seeking sleep. The occasional bleak sound of a distant foghorn echoing from somewhere gave me a feeling of loneliness and isolation I'd never experienced before. It made me aware that this cottage was a long way from the main house and there was no means of communication if . . .

If what? I demanded of myself irritably, thumping the pillow, and burrowing deeper under the quilt. *Go to sleep!* I ordered myself, fighting the beginnings of a vague uneasiness.

I woke from a dream-troubled sleep and lay very still for a few minutes. I thought I heard footsteps moving in the outer room, even though I knew that was impossible. I'd latched the door behind me when I'd come in, I was sure. I felt a ripple of apprehension at the base of my skull, and my heart quickened its beat perceptibly. *This is ridiculous,* I told myself. *You're imagining it.* It was probably the night sounds in the woods surrounding the cottage, the sighs and whispers of the wind high up in the tall cedars, or even the sound of the far-off surf. I snuggled into the blankets, willing myself to go back to sleep. But I couldn't right away, and I lay awake thinking once more of the strange events I'd heard about yesterday from Jeff Maxwell, about the tragic death of the first Mrs. Bradford and its aftermath. There was an aura of mystery, a psychic residue of violence, tragedy, and horror about Gull's Glen, and I'd picked up on it. Had it been a tragic accident or an unsolved murder?

In spite of my determination not to, I was becoming involved in the past events and present conflicts at Gull's Glen.

The light became gray in my room as dawn crept in and I finally fell back to sleep.

CHAPTER 9

I awakened to a room full of sunlight. I jumped out of bed and looked out the window. Last night's nagging fear dissolved with the view of the sparkling sea and cloudless blue sky. A wonderful day to begin the sittings, I thought, as I hurried to dress and make coffee before Dortha arrived.

Dortha came dressed in a simple pastel-striped blouse, lilac cardigan, and matching slacks. She wore sandals and carried a canvas tote bag with her initials on it.

She looked lovely, but as soon as she walked in, I knew it was going to be hard getting her to relax. Her movements were jerky, and when I tried having her sit on the comfortable sofa, she still held herself rigidly.

When she reached for the mug of coffee I offered, her

hand shook noticeably. I fought the hopeless feeling that surged up inside me. *My first big commission and the subject is putting up all kinds of barriers to my success,* I thought desperately. What could I do to combat Dortha's inner tension?

Almost as if she caught my anxiety, Dortha put out her hand to touch my arm impulsively and said, "Don't worry, Miss Forrest, I'll calm down in a few minutes. I met Aaron on the way down here and we—well, it upset me a little, I'm afraid." She looked anxious. "He's so terribly hostile . . ." Her voice trailed off into a sigh.

"I'm sorry," I said, "but it's not your fault. He's like a lot of young people his age, mad at the world. He has a lot of feelings he can't quite control; he's still got a lot of growing up to do."

"I wish that were all there was to it. You don't understand how he feels about . . . me and his father. I'm just so worried he'll . . ." Again her voice lowered until it was almost a whisper.

"I'm sorry. This has nothing to do with you. I shouldn't bother you with our troubles. Now, how and where do you want me to sit?"

"Let's just sit here on the couch and talk for a while. I'd like to get to know you a little better, and have you feel comfortable with me. We won't do anything formal today. I'll just make some sketches while we chat, okay? And by the way, please call me Cam," I said.

"If you'll call me Dortha," she answered quickly.

Dortha adjusted some pillows behind her and settled back against them. I got my sketch pad and sat at the other end of the couch, and started talking about the movies that had won the Academy Awards this year. Since they'd been out of the country most of the year, Dortha said, she hadn't seen any of the current films, and she began asking me about some I'd seen and enjoyed.

We must have talked quietly for about a half an hour as I sketched. I saw Dortha becoming more at ease. She was so lovely this morning, even with no makeup, and in her simple outfit, that it was a pleasure to look at her and draw. As she talked about some of the places they had been in Europe, her face became more animated and I realized why Justin was so anxious to have her painted. The only flaw I could see was her nervousness. It remained there, just under the surface, sabotaging what should be a serene beauty. Her smile, for example, was beautiful, worth waiting to catch, but it came and went so quickly, leaving that frightened expression on her face.

At the moment when Dortha was telling me about shopping for Dresden china in Holland, I was sketching as rapidly as I could when, looking up, I suddenly saw her face undergo a complete change. For no apparent reason she halted mid-sentence. Her eyes widened and glazed, her mouth began to tremble. She was looking past me over my shoulder.

Automatically I turned to look in the direction into which Dortha stared. I saw nothing but a movement that might have been simply a shadow passing over the sun, for there was no one by the window.

She went white; the color seemed to drain completely from her face. The fear in her expression darkened her eyes and wiped away completely that sweet serenity I so longed to paint.

She got up abruptly and ran over to the window. When she turned back into the room, she looked pale, as though she might faint.

"What's the matter, Dortha, are you feeling ill?" I asked, getting up and going toward her.

She put both hands tremblingly up to her temples and swayed slightly.

"What? Ill? No, no, it's just . . ."

"Shall I get you some more coffee or maybe some tea?" I put my hand on her arm. "Why don't you come over and sit down and let me fix a pot of tea—"

"Have you—anything stronger?" she asked hesitantly. "I am feeling a little weak."

"There's some brandy. Wait, I'll get it."

I went over to the decanter on the table, filled a glass and took it to her. She practically gulped it down. Gradually some color came back into her face. She got up then and fumbled in her tote bag and brought out a pack of cigarettes. She took a long filtered one out and lighted it with a slim gold lighter, inhaled deeply and blew out the smoke, then began to pace up and down the room.

"Justin hates me to smoke, but I started in order to keep my weight down when I was modeling—it's hard to quit. I really don't think I can sit any longer today. I'm getting a horrible headache . . . just like the other night. I think I'll go walk along the beach, get some fresh air."

With that she crushed out her cigarette in one of the large shell ashtrays on an end table, looked at me with wide eyes filled with some unspeakable fear, and whispered huskily, "I'm sorry. It's all so impossible." Then she turned away and said nothing else, grabbed up her bag and started toward the door.

"Same time tomorrow, Dortha?"

She hesitated, her hand on the doorknob, not turning back. She did not answer and at first I thought she might not have heard me so I repeated the question.

There was a deep sigh.

"Oh, Cam—I don't know."

Her voice carried such a note of desperation that I was stunned. I saw Dortha's slim shoulders slump momentarily, then she opened the door and went out.

From the window I could see her walk rapidly across the little bridge, hesitate for a minute, then turn toward the path that led to the sea walk and to the beach.

"Well, that's that for the day," I said aloud, packing away my sketch pad, replacing my soft drawing pencils in the container near my easel in the alcove by the large window.

It had been a strange session at best. The ground I'd gained with Dortha had been lost by whatever or whoever she had seen outside my window.

CHAPTER 10

With our sitting so abruptly ended by Dortha's departure, I had the rest of the day to myself. I had not expected to have this much time to myself when I came to Gull's Glen. I had anticipated sittings in the morning, blocking in and painting most of the afternoons. But then neither had I expected all the strange situations I'd encountered there.

It was a beautiful day and I decided to explore the beach. I took along my sketch pad and some colored pens, planning to do some drawings that I could possibly turn into paintings later.

I started putting my things in my basket, then remembered I had promised to call Aunt Mim and let her know how things were coming along. I would certainly have to make things sound better than they actually were. Leaving my basket of supplies to be picked up later, I took the path through the woods up to the house.

As I emerged from the clearing at the edge of the woods, the house and driveway came into sight. As I neared them, I was surprised to see Justin standing on the steps with Ennis Shelby.

I hesitated, not wanting to interrupt, but I had come too far to turn back. Besides, just as I'd seen them, Justin, then Ennis, turned in my direction. Since they'd both seen me, there was nothing to do but continue walking toward the house.

As I came up to where they stood, Justin spoke. "Sitting

finished so soon? Where's Dortha? I didn't see her come up."

I explained she wanted to walk on the beach for a while.

A puzzled frown creased Justin's broad forehead for a minute, then he said, "Excuse me, my dear, may I introduce Ennis Shelby. This is our guest, Miss Cameron Forrest."

"We've already met, Justin, in town yesterday at Maxwell's shop. And how goes the portrait?" he asked pleasantly enough, but I saw him cast a quick glance at Justin, who reacted by a flush and a tightening of his lips.

"Off to a good start, I think," I replied evenly, hoping to avoid any more questions. I turned to Justin and asked, "May I use the phone to call my aunt in San Francisco? I'll reverse the charges of course."

"Certainly, go right ahead. There are two extensions downstairs, one in my study, the other in the small den opposite the living room. Feel free to use the phone any time. And do give my regards to your aunt, won't you?"

My conversation with Aunt Mim lasted a little over five minutes. I told her about my lovely cottage, the scenery, and that I'd started working on Dortha's portrait. She was so happy and enthusiastic at my report and had no idea of all I was not telling her. We exchanged some family news. I told her I would keep in touch and then we hung up.

When I came back out on the terrace, Justin and Ennis were still standing there. They both turned at my approach.

"Make your call all right?" Justin asked.

"Yes, thank you." I started to walk past them. "Since our sitting is over for today, I think I'll explore the beach some more."

"Wait a minute, Miss Forrest. I'll walk down with you," Ennis Shelby said. "I'm going home anyway. Thank you, Justin, for your okay. I'll try not to disturb anyone."

"That's all right, Ennis," Justin replied, although I did

not think his tone was hearty or friendly. "Oh, if you see Dortha," he called after us, "tell her I'm waiting lunch for her."

"Terribly possessive of her, isn't he?" Ennis remarked in a low tone as we started down the path. "The poor girl can't even take a solo walk without him sending out a scouting party!"

I made no comment. I certainly wasn't going to express an opinion on my employer as well as my host to a man I barely knew.

My lack of response was noted, for Ennis gave a short laugh and said, "Sorry. Of course you can't say anything, no matter what you observe. That was tactless of me. Forgive me. It's just that I hope Justin doesn't make the same mistake with his new wife that he made with Rosalind—" He paused. "I hope he's learned that you can't cage a free spirit . . . be it a bird or a woman."

Although I was curious to know how Ennis knew so much about Justin and Rosalind Bradford, and wondered how close a friend he was before the tragedy, I could not bring myself to ask a leading question just to satisfy my curiosity. There were so many puzzling things about the people at Gull's Glen. Still, it wasn't for me to probe, even though Ennis Shelby seemed inclined to talk.

We stopped briefly at my cottage to pick up my basket of art supplies. Ennis waited on the doorstep and when I came back out he said in a speculative tone, "It's really strange they'd give you the same cottage. Of course, the ocean window provides a good light, but all the same . . . I think it's most odd."

This time I couldn't resist asking, "What do you mean?"

"Of course, you wouldn't know, but this is the cottage Cole Burnham used when he was painting Rosalind's portrait—the one he was doing when she—died."

An involuntary shudder went through me. Ennis noticed and said immediately, "Perhaps I shouldn't have told you. It's just that it struck me as a little macabre since both of them . . . are dead. It shouldn't bother you at all, of course. It's just that knowing them both so well, I just couldn't help but think . . ." He stopped. "I must apologize. I haven't been back here since it all happened, and I guess it was all at once—very poignant."

It was impossible not to ask, "Then you were here when it happened, when Rosalind—"

"No, actually not when it happened. I was in San Francisco. I had a show opening, so I was away at the time. But Cole Burnham was staying at my cottage . . . that is, after Justin threw him out."

I stopped in my tracks and stared at him.

"Oh, Justin was having one of his periodic jealousy attacks, thought that Cole and Rosalind were becoming too close during the portrait sittings. He was jealous of any man that came near her, actually. I can see why this time he commissioned a woman artist to paint his wife." There was heavy sarcasm in the last remark.

"You mean he asked this Cole Burnham to leave with the portrait not finished?" I asked.

"Yes. As I understand it, there was a dreadful row. Of course I heard all this second-hand, but by then . . . well, Rosalind was dead."

"How sad," I commented.

"More than sad. The whole thing need never have occurred, if Justin had just controlled his unreasonable temper. When Cole tried to come back, collect his things, Justin threatened him and pushed him around. Cole wasn't as big physically as Justin, and I guess there was another scene. I don't blame Cole. It was an irrational thing for Justin to do in the first place, then equally unjustified not to let Cole back on the property. Cole had left several hundred dollars' worth of painting equipment in the cottage, and, of course, the half-finished portrait."

We had come to the bridge arching over the shallow stream, and we stood there for a few minutes listening to the soft, musical sound of the water rippling over the smooth flat rocks. It was so peaceful, so tranquil that I wondered how it could have been the scene of such violence as Ennis had just described.

"I don't know anywhere else where you have this curious combination of quiet forest and then only a short distance away the entirely different, but just as spectacular, ocean scenery. That's why I asked Justin if I could prowl around here for the next week or so getting some photographs. It's truly magnificent, isn't it?"

He had changed the subject and I was glad. My mind was too full of the Bradfords and their emotionally charged lives. I wanted to have an afternoon clear of other people's problems, a few hours in which to indulge my creativity in this beautiful place.

We had reached the sea path and walked together to the top of the wooden stairway leading down the cliffs to the cove. Ennis was behind me, and as I started to take hold of the railing, something stopped me. An emotion I could not name gripped me with an unreasonable sense of danger.

I looked down to where the surf was crashing against the cliffs and felt dizzy. It was a long way down. Suddenly I tensed. I couldn't go forward, and yet I was too paralyzed with fear to turn around toward Ennis. Why? I couldn't explain it. In another moment his hand grasped my elbow firmly, and he said in a calm voice, "It is a little frightening from this height, but I'll hold you until you get your footing. Don't be afraid."

I turned and looked at him then. His smile was reassuring—and very attractive.

Irrelevantly I thought, *He's very handsome.* As quickly as it had come, that moment of panic disappeared. With Ennis's firm hold and my basket of art supplies balanced, I descended the rickety steps with no further difficulty.

When we reached the bottom, our feet sank into the soft sand, and Ennis swore softly under his breath.

"I don't know why in the devil Justin doesn't have those steps repaired or torn out and new ones built. They're slippery as hell when it's wet, and after all that's happened, you'd think he'd at least do that."

The frown that brought his heavy brows together soon smoothed out as he smiled at me again.

"Well, have a happy afternoon. If you feel like it, when you're finished sketching, why not stop by my place and have a drink. It's right over there." He pointed to a slanted roof barely visible above the dunes to the left of the steps. "Do come, I'd really like it if you would."

Not waiting for my answer, he gave me his characteristic salute, turned away, and walked down the beach toward his cottage.

To be truthful, I was flattered by his invitation, even though I wasn't sure at the moment whether or not to accept it.

After all, from what Jeff Maxwell had said, Ennis Shelby had a prestigious reputation as a photographer and probably moved in the sophisticated art and social circles of San Francisco. Add this to that fact that he was obviously a man of the world, at least ten years older than I, as well as being handsome and attractive. There would be some risk involved in getting to know Ennis Shelby, I thought. But then, all new experiences have a risk factor. I'd just wait and see how my afternoon went before deciding.

CHAPTER 11

As it turned out, I did not do much sketching. After a few attempts I put aside my sketch pad and pencils and sprawled on my stomach staring out at the sea. The sun on the water was dazzling and watching the waves rush in and out in swirls of lacy foam on the brown sugar sand was hypnotizing. The cliffs above the beach where the yellow and purple lupine clung were a tapestry of color against the gray rocks. The gulls dipping and calling, the shorebirds doing a patterned ballet at the ocean's edge all had a lulling effect. The afternoon simply spun away in a sort of golden trance.

Maybe this was just what I needed, I told myself indulgently, a quiet, relaxing time untroubled with plans or speculations about other people's problems.

After a long while I could tell from the position of the sun that it was growing late. Reluctantly I gathered up my things, put them back in the basket, folded my blanket, and stood up.

I looked toward the gray, weathered cottage at the end of the inlet and wondered if I should take Ennis up on his invitation. Not finding any reason not to, I decided to go. A few minutes later I found myself at the bright blue door sheltered by a latticed arch, my hand raised to knock. On either side of the entrance were the biggest geranium bushes I'd ever seen, crowded with red and pink blooms.

In answer to my second knock the door opened, and Ennis, in a black turtleneck sweater and jeans, beckoned me inside with a broad smile.

"Hello! I wasn't sure you'd come," he greeted me.

"Why not?" I asked surprised, wondering if my hesitancy about accepting his invitation had been that obvious.

"Oh, because you seem to be a very determined young lady. That is to say, you had planned to go to the beach and sketch and nothing was going to deter you. But I'm glad to see you came."

"You're quite wrong about me, you know. I did hardly any sketching. Most of the time I just lay in the sun and—did nothing."

"I'm relieved to hear you're not such a paragon of

virtue as I thought at first," Ennis said. "What will you have to drink, white wine, sherry, or . . . ?"

"White wine, please."

Although Ennis had referred to his house as a beach shack, as soon as I stepped inside I saw it was hardly that.

My first impression was of uncluttered order and nicely defined space. It reflected the owner's taste and style in an understated way which was original, personal, and comfortable.

The floor was bare, except for some black and white woven rugs—Peruvian design, I thought. There was a modular sectional sofa covered in some rough-textured off-white material, strewn with dozens of bright pillows. On either side of the fireplace of white painted brick were floor to ceiling bookcases. Over the mantel was an excellent seascape and on the white plaster walls were several handsomely framed black and white photographs.

A room divider separated the living room from what I could see of a white and chrome, thoroughly modern kitchen. Along the sea side of the house were windows, across which, after bringing me my wine, Ennis was pulling rust-colored curtains.

Ennis plumped up the sofa cushions invitingly and motioned me to sit down. He took a seat opposite me on the other couch and raised his glass.

"To the successful completion of your—task," he said. "I earnestly hope a happier conclusion to the painting of the portrait of *this* Mrs. Bradford."

I took a sip of the wine, not saying anything in reply, but thinking there was some reason for Ennis to bring up the subject of Rosalind Bradford again. Was there a reason, perhaps, for inviting me here? After a minute, I asked, "Did you know Rosalind Bradford well?"

"I met them both when I first bought this place," Ennis said. "They used to walk on the beach almost every day with the dogs and one of the first mornings I was here they came by." He paused thoughtfully. "They came to welcome me, actually. Rosalind was a delightful person, very open, very friendly. She said she had seen the smoke coming from the chimney and was so glad someone was living here, as the cottage had been empty a long time, and it would be nice to have neighbors. Justin, I must admit, was not quite so enthusiastic. He valued his privacy then as much as he does now. Anyway, that's how I met Rosalind. Actually I got to know her better than Justin. Justin just doesn't care about enlarging his circle of friends. But Rosalind . . . was different. People fascinated her. Maybe it was the actress in her. She wanted to know about you, what you thought, did, dreamed about, wanted out of life . . . everything!"

"Her death must have been a terrible shock to everyone," I said.

Ennis leaned forward to jab at the open fire with a poker.

"Yes, a terrible shock," he repeated. "It's hard to think of Rosalind being dead.

"I never knew anyone more alive than Rosalind. She was strong and vibrant, full of warmth and laughter, outgoing and vivacious. She had what they call joie de vivre. You couldn't help but feel happier just to be around her. Everyone reacted to Rosalind that way."

I was startled to see Ennis's face as he spoke of Rosalind. It seemed more angry than sad talking about the death of his friend. A moment of silence hung between us. Then, with a quick smile Ennis said, "But as the poet has said, 'What's gone and what's past help, should be past grief . . .' " He paused. "So, tell me, what do you think of the household at Gull's Glen. Bianca's rather formidable, isn't she? And those two maverick children. I imagine Justin hasn't been able to corral them yet. I see them wandering all over the cliffs like two ragamuffin gypsies. For all their fine foreign schooling I doubt they're tamable."

"I really haven't had a chance to get to know them," I answered.

I didn't think I should discuss the Bradfords with Ennis. If he knew them so well, why did he ask so many questions about them? As if sensing my reluctance, Ennis switched the subject to his request to tramp the woods surrounding the Bradford house and of the exhibit he was planning to do of photos of this part of the California coast.

"You know, it's totally unique." He launched into an animated explanation of his plans and his hopes for this particular project.

It was clear that Ennis loved his profession. As he talked, I changed my first impression of him as a cool, aloof, rather blasé person. Instead, Ennis now seemed to be warm, enthusiastic, amusing. He was knowledgeable about all the arts, asking me intelligent questions about my work, and he knew some of the contemporary artists I most admired as well. I was enjoying myself, completely unaware of the time, until Ennis suggested, "More wine?"

"Oh, no, I really should be going," I said, glancing at my watch. "Dinner is at seven and I have to bathe and change—" I got up.

"Must you go? I could grill us a couple of steaks. Couldn't you stay? I'm really enjoying our conversation," Ennis said.

"Thank you, but no."

"Another time?"

"I'd like that."

"I have to go to San Francisco for a few days, but I'll contact you when I get back and we'll set a definite date for you to have dinner here."

He walked with me to the door.

"I'd like to show you some of the photographs I took a few years ago. There are some of Rosalind, incidentally, which would be interesting for you. They are some I took for Cole in preparation for his portrait of her. That's not, of course, the only reason I'd like you to come, you know. I just thought it might appeal to your professional interest, since you told me you sometimes work from photographs as well as sketches."

"Good, I'll look forward to it."

He opened the door for me then, and peered out. "Uh-oh, fog's coming in. Would you like me to see you up the steps back to your cottage?"

"Oh, no thanks, that's not necessary," I said.

"Wait, don't forget your basket," he said, reaching down and picking it up from where I'd left it just inside the front door.

"Thanks for a very pleasant time," I said, starting out.

"My pleasure," he called after me.

The fog was rolling in fast, swirling around me as I hurried toward the rickety stairs leading up from the beach. It was getting dark, and when I reached the bottom of the steps and looked back, Ennis's cottage had all but disappeared in the murky fog.

I began scuttling up the steps, stumbling a little once in a while on a loose board, an uneven ridge. Ennis was right. This stairway was in dreadful condition. It could be dangerous, too, especially coming down. If your heel should get caught, you'd tumble down and possibly get hurt badly. I was breathless when I finally reached the top. By this time the fog was really thick. Ghostly wisps curled around the trees in smoky tendrils as I started down the wooded path toward the guest cottage.

Without any warning, there was a loud crashing of underbrush and a huge animal leaped into the path in front of me. I let out a strangled scream, and jumped back, losing my balance, thrusting one hand in front of me to ward off the attack, the other clutching to steady myself on the rough side of a tree. My heart was thundering inside of me.

"Bruno, halt!" came the command issued by a young male voice.

The roaring bark diminished to a throaty snarl. I clung weakly to the tree as two figures emerged from the fog. It was Aaron and one of the Weimaraners.

The dog obeyed instantly, and halted.

When I could manage to speak, I gasped, "You really frightened me."

"Miss Forrest? What are you doing out here at this time . . . in the dark?" Aaron's voice sounded puzzled.

"I was coming up from the beach—" I began.

"I'm sorry. I thought you were a trespasser. Bruno's trained to attack."

I took a long, shaky breath.

"I'm glad you were with him."

Now the dog was making little whimpering noises.

"It's all right, Bruno. Let him come toward you. He'll recognize your scent, then everything will be okay," Aaron said.

"You're sure—?" I asked hesitantly.

"Positive. Okay, Bruno."

The big dog came up to me, his tail wagging now, his warm, rough tongue licking my hand. I let out my breath slowly. I put out my hand, stroked his broad head, and I could feel his weight as he leaned against me.

"Sorry," Aaron said again awkwardly, then, "Come, Bruno," and he brushed past me without a word.

My breath was still shallow when I reached my cottage. I opened the door, closed it, set down my basket, and leaned against the door breathing deeply, trying to calm my still-pounding heart.

I rather dreaded going up to the house for dinner that night, but a quick look at my watch warned me I'd have to hurry. I was sure Bianca would not appreciate my being late and I also knew that Justin enjoyed making a ritual out of the cocktail hour.

I took a quick shower and dressed. I didn't have time to savor the unexpectedly pleasurable visit with Ennis Shelby.

For some reason the fog did not seem as thick when I set out from the cottage. Using my powerful flashlight, I made my way easily along the wooded path. Lights were streaming out from every window, and as soon as I came to the edge of the lawn, I clicked off the torch.

I let myself in the front door, as I'd been urged to come and go as a member of the household by both Justin and Bianca. I was just crossing the front hall to the drawing room when I heard voices raised in anger. My hand was stretched out to turn the knob of the paneled door when I heard Bianca saying, "You're the one that's being unreasonable."

"For God's sake, Bianca, can't you allow anyone to be happy?" That was Justin.

I turned around and started to recross the hall and slam the front door or something to announce my arrival, when I looked up and saw Dortha coming down the stairway. There was nothing to do except use her to let the others know I was here. In an unusually loud tone of voice I greeted her, "Well, Dortha, your walk on the beach seems to have done you a world of good. Your color is beautiful tonight!"

"Yes, I'm feeling much better," she replied.

I felt relieved. I saw a glimmer of a smile and Dortha's whole manner seemed less tense.

My ploy worked, for immediately the drawing room door opened and Justin looked out. His glance barely grazed me but went straight to Dortha. *He really is madly in love with her,* I thought with a tinge of envy.

Dinner was better than I'd anticipated. Perhaps without the presence of the two sullen youngsters, everyone felt more relaxed. Whatever argument had been going on between Justin and Bianca before dinner, there was no evidence of it now. The conversation flowed easily and everyone seemed to be making a special effort. It was only when Justin asked me how the morning's sitting had gone that I tensed. Automatically I looked at Dortha, who sent me an anxious, pleading look. I knew she was silently begging me not to tell how she had abruptly ended the session before it had begun. I tried to reassure her that I had no intention of doing so, and explained to Justin that sometimes the preliminary sketches take a while, but are very important to the decisions the artist has to make about the composition of the portrait.

"After that, the actual painting goes surprisingly fast," I told him.

This seemed to satisfy him, and he suggested we all go into the drawing room for coffee and liqueur. As soon as I reasonably could, I pleaded tiredness after my afternoon of sun and sea air and said good night.

Again Bianca accompanied me to the front door. As she opened it, we saw that a light rain was falling.

"Here, you better wear this or you'll be soaked before you get inside the cottage." She reached behind the door to a row of coat hooks and brought out a long, hooded cape. "This is wonderfully warm. Rosalind brought it back from Ireland. It's wool tweed. It'll keep you completely dry. You can just bring it back with you in the morning. It always hangs here for anyone to use."

As she held it for me and I felt its light warmth cover me, I couldn't help remembering that eerie figure I'd seen in the pre-dawn the first morning I awoke at Gull's Glen. If this cape were available to anyone, who had passed so stealthily by my window and who had been walking on the beach later? It could have been anyone.

CHAPTER 12

The next few days were relatively uneventful. The daily work of the portrait took on a sort of pattern.

Dortha came about ten for her sitting, and as she became more at ease with me, the sketching went well. I thought I now had the right pose for her and began blocking in the rough outlines on the canvas I'd already primed and prepared with ocher and white. I was getting the kind of spontaneous feeling I liked and I became more enthusiastic about the ultimate success of the portrait.

Dortha's features were so perfect, her coloring so lovely, that it was a challenge to paint her with a light touch so as not to lose the delicacy. She was like a Romney lady and my aim was to create a portrait reminiscent of that master's style, but in a contemporary setting.

We discussed the dress Justin was insisting Dortha be painted in and together agreed we'd finish this one first, then do a more formal sitting to please him.

"We won't say anything yet, or let him see this one," I suggested. "Then, when he sees both paintings, he can decide which one he wants. It's no loss to me. I can always include the one you don't decide on in an exhibit," I told Dortha.

Now that I knew her taste in music—show tunes, themes from movies, ballads—I played tapes I thought she'd like on the stereo. It relaxed her and gave her face the dreamy quality I was trying for. We took breaks twice an hour and a longer one in the middle of the three-hour session to have coffee, sweet rolls, and to chat. The more we talked, the better I liked Dortha. She began to regard me as a friend.

During one of these times Dortha told me how she met Justin.

"It was in New York. Like thousands of other small-town girls I'd gone there with the idea of being a model, leading a glamorous, luxurious life. You see, I'd always been considered pretty in high school, won a local beauty contest, that sort of thing. And I was so naive, so sheltered, people were always telling me I ought to be a model, so I thought I could be one." Dortha shook her head. "I can't believe I was so dumb. I didn't realize that all those other girls streaming in from all over the United States from other small towns were just as pretty, or prettier, and were just as eager to make it big in the city as I was. I had no idea of the competition you face. I mean, for one tiny modeling job maybe two hundred girls show up . . . all so gorgeous you begin to feel tacky, ugly, and awful just looking around you. Well, I'd arrived in New York with just under eight hundred dollars so you can imagine how long that lasted, and I panicked. I didn't feel I could go back home and face people with the fact that I hadn't made it. So I did what I told myself would be temporary. Luckily I'd taken a business course in school, so I could type and take shorthand. I signed up with one of those agencies that send you out to work in various offices for vacation relief for their regular secretarial help. This way I could pay my rent, eat, and try to get a portfolio together. You have no idea what photographers charge for the glossies the agencies demand you have if they take you on as one of their models. Well, I stuck it out for over a year, but it was grim. Between office jobs, I trudged around from agency to agency, then went out for the auditions they'd send me on. My taxi fares alone . . . because most of the time I didn't have time to spend on buses or go through the hassle of the subways. Besides, I was scared riding them. I had one or two dreadful experiences!" She sighed. "I just wasn't cut out for big city life, but I did try. Oh, boy, did I try . . ."

A strange, rather sad expression clouded her face for a moment. "The things girls are expected to do—to put up with—to get started modeling, you wouldn't believe! The stuff you swallow, it just made me sick. I was getting pretty disillusioned, pretty turned off men—" here a smile played around the corners of her mouth "—when I met Justin. He was so different. He treated me with such—respect, I guess you'd say. I was just blown away!"

"But how did you meet him?" I asked.

"Justin was in New York on his way to Europe. He was in consultation with his publishers about the book he'd just finished. Well, they wanted some last-minute revisions, some minor changes, so he called the secretarial service I was signed up with for a secretary, and it just so happened I was in the office when he called and they sent me over to his hotel." She shrugged. "I guess you'd call it kismet, fate, or karma, whatever."

"Justin tells me he fell in love with me the minute I walked into the room." Dortha gave a soft little laugh. "It wasn't like that for me. Frankly I didn't know who he was. I'd never read one of his books, never even heard of him. Isn't that awful! I just never read much. Anyway, I was a little nervous, always am, starting a new job. But he was so gracious, so considerate, so—well, you know how wonderful Justin is. That first day he ordered lunch for us, room service . . . I'd never had such an elaborate lunch. He treated me with such dignity. Oh, I don't know, I was just overwhelmed. The revisions and changes he'd told his publishers would take him maybe a week took him three weeks. I was there every day, but we didn't work very much. He always had some plan, someplace he wanted to take me, something he wanted me to see . . . restaurants, museums, the theater. It was like some kind of fairy tale for me. Then he bought me this ring." Dortha held up her hand, the huge emerald glittering in the sunlight. "And asked me to marry him. I was with him when he finally left for Europe.

"We were going to Greece—Justin was doing research for the background of his new book—but first we went to London, then to France. It was heaven!" Dortha paused, smiling as she thought of her happy memories. "That is, until Paris . . ."

"Paris! I should think Paris would be the peak experience of a first trip to Europe. Didn't you like it?" I asked, surprised.

"Oh, Paris itself was marvelous—beyond what you could imagine. But the children . . . Aaron and Olivia, met us there. Justin had sent them a long telegram telling them of our marriage and arranging for them to come to Paris to join us for what was to be a wonderful week of getting to know each other and having fun together as a family. Justin had planned so many things, but it was a disaster."

I didn't need to ask why. Dortha went on.

"From the moment they got off the plane from Switzerland, it was terrible. They made no effort whatsoever and did everything to sabotage Justin's plans. They were outright rude and hostile to me, and it made Justin furious. It ended up by him putting them back on the plane to return to their school. That was a relief, of course, but that part of our trip was ruined. The bad taste of it lingered for a long time. It wasn't until we'd been at the house Justin rented for us on one of the islands that we began to find each other again. Up until then he'd been all tied up with worry, resentment, and guilt. A barrier I couldn't get through." She took a long breath. "There it was just idyllic. We were so in love, Justin's work went well, we spent long days together in the sun, sight-seeing, swimming. Everything was perfect until Justin said we had to come back here.

"Of course, Justin had told me about his first marriage . . . the tragedy . . . all of it. I didn't see why he would want to come back here to the scene of all his unhappiness and trauma. But he said it was the only place he could put a book together. Besides, it was the children's home, and their school holidays were coming up and it was imperative that we all be together as a family."

Dortha lit a cigarette, took a long draw on it, and sighed.

"Of course, I knew the children would be difficult, but it might have been possible if it hadn't been for Bianca." She gave a little shudder. She paused as if she were trying to decide whether to go on or not. Evidently she thought it was safe to confide in me, for she spoke in a flat, expressionless tone.

"I hadn't met Bianca until we arrived here. She lives here all the time, you see, while Justin is usually only here from May until October. So in a way, she feels this is her house, her *home*, and she made me feel like—an unwelcome guest." Another pause. "She hates me with a dull and bitter hatred. Maybe she would feel that way about anyone Justin married after Rosalind, I don't know. I am the . . . the outsider, the unwanted replacement for her sister. Did you know she keeps one of these cottages like a shrine to Rosalind? All of her things—clothes, books, scrapbooks, pictures . . . everything, just as though she were still alive." Again she shuddered. "Sometimes I think she still is alive!"

We didn't get much done after that. Dortha seemed nervous and couldn't maintain her pose. Finally I suggested we stop for the day.

That frightened, haunted look had come into Dortha's expression again after she had talked about Bianca. Was Bianca jealous of her sister's memory, resentful of anyone who tried to usurp her place? Or was it Dortha's overactive imagination? There was a strange atmosphere at Gull's Glen, a sort of pervasive unease. I had felt it almost from the first and the tension and hostility among the members of the family was very real. Was there some kind of conspiracy to destroy Justin's happiness with Dortha? Dortha was afraid of something or someone. Was someone out to destroy her marriage?

I cleaned my brushes, covered my palette, and put a drop cloth over the easel.

I felt frustrated. I had had a good momentum going today and had not wanted to stop. Portrait painting involves an artist completely. Many times when I was in portrait class at the Art Institute I had felt this same kind of restless frustration when the class ended, the model gone. My instructor had warned me that the very intensity with which I painted could be a problem.

I knew that this was happening with Dortha Bradford, reflected in the very fact that I wanted to paint her twice—once as I saw her honestly, and again as her husband wanted her idealized. I knew there were actually two Dorthas, the real one, and the other person she allowed the world to see.

"If you're going into portrait painting as a career, Cam," my instructor cautioned me, "try to put your brush aside before you go too far. Your client may not be happy with the results if you penetrate beneath the public face to that hidden self that only they know about."

In Dortha's case I would have to be especially careful. I didn't want to paint the fear I saw in her eyes.

I fixed myself a sandwich and a glass of iced tea, then got a sweater and put on sneakers. In the last few days I had got into the habit of going to the beach in the afternoons after we finished our sitting. It was so beautiful, and I found it refreshing, renewing after a morning of intense work.

I didn't bother to take along a sketch pad. I realized from that first day that it just became baggage. It was better for me to just go and reenergize myself by walking in the sand, shell-hunting, or simply basking in the sun and sea air.

Today, especially, I needed to leave my work behind, to forget the tangled affairs at the Bradford mansion and the problems I was having with Dortha's portrait.

I took the path through the woods that joined the seawall path, but I had not walked far when I got the distinct feeling I was being followed.

CHAPTER 13

I stopped, instinctively listening. The woods seemed very still, very silent. It was just a feeling I had, a sudden prickling sensation along my scalp, a quick shiver along my spine, an unreasonable quickening of my heartbeat. I waited a minute, but nothing happened. I took a tentative step or two forward. Then behind me I heard the snapping of a twig. I whirled around just in time to see a quick, darting movement behind a tree a yard or so back of me.

It was so fast I couldn't be sure, but I thought I saw a flash of long red-gold hair.

I took a chance. I walked forward to where I thought I saw a shadow and called, "Olivia! Olivia, is that you?"

I halted. There was no answer, no sound. I waited. In another minute, the small, slim figure of Justin's daughter, in denim cutoffs and an old gray sweat shirt with the sleeves raggedly torn, stepped out from behind one of the large cedars, a sheepish expression on her face.

"Want to walk down to the beach with me?" I asked casually, making no mention of the fact that she had been tracking me like some kind of spy.

She stood there awkwardly, thumbs hooked into the worn pockets of her shorts. Then, with a toss of that glorious hair, she shrugged and ambled toward me.

"Okay," she said indifferently.

I turned and started walking again toward the seawall path. She fell into step beside me, then said, "I know a shortcut. It's kind of a secret way to the beach, but there's a neat—come on, I'll show you," she said with some animation in her voice now.

She went ahead, running lightly along the fern-banked path that wound above the cliffs hazed with the purplish-blue of lupine growing among the rocks. I followed. The path seemed to take us away from the direction of the ocean but finally, when I scrambled after Olivia up on a knoll, I saw where she was leading. At the top was a glass-enclosed vista point with benches and a table out of the wind, a sun-warmed place from which there was a spectacular view of the whole beach.

Olivia turned to me expectantly.

"Isn't this neat? I just love being up here. My mother had it built. She used to bring us, Aaron and me, up here on picnics lots of times when we were little. There is a path down to the cove where it's safe to swim. There's no other place, except our secret inlet, where it's safe for swimming, and there only at low tide."

I was breathless from trying to keep up with her as she had leaped from rock to ridge like a young deer. It felt good to sit in the sun-warmed enclosure and drink in the spectacular view of sky and sea for as far as you could see. The air was moist with the tang of salt and the smell of seaweed. I felt exhilarated as I watched the ocean below us. A large wave crested and crashed furiously, fanning out foam-edged semicircles, sending hundreds of little rivulets spilling onto the sand.

"Do you still come here often?" I asked.

"We used to come all the time when my mother was alive," Olivia said, her young face suddenly pensive. "But we go to school in Switzerland and just come here summers now. Aaron and I are the only ones that know about it, except my father. But he never comes anymore now that Mother's dead. It makes him sad to be reminded of her in any way. That's why, I think, he doesn't like to have me around too much. Did you know I look very much like her? Aunt Bianca says so. I'd like to be an actress like my mother, but my father gets furious if I say anything about it. Aunt Bianca says I could be . . . that is, if I am willing to sacrifice for it. It takes more than being beautiful, you know. Years of training and discipline. But my father won't let me go to drama school. He's already said so. Out of the question. Never!" She sighed.

The way all this was pouring out of her in such a rush to me, I realized that Olivia had been starved for someone to talk to, someone who would listen to her. I also realized that the attitude she had assumed the times I'd seen her at the dinner table was an act. She was a very good actress, I thought. The talkative, animated child I was seeing now was a far cry from the sulky one I had seen then. Was it Aaron who had been directing their "act," dictating Olivia's demeanor? Away from her brother, released from whatever dictum he had issued on their unified behavior for their father's benefit, she was a far different person, one I could like, I thought. Underneath her rather brittle front was a very vulnerable, lonely little girl.

"Let's go down and look in the tide pools," she suggested, jumping up and, without waiting for my agreement, starting down an almost hidden path through the rocks to the beach below.

Olivia knew the beach well. She knew the names of all the little sea creatures that lived in the tide pools and the birds that lived by the shore. Just listening to her, I learned more in one afternoon than I had learned in my one term of marine biology at college.

As well as being knowledgeable, she was acutely aware. Even when I was completely fascinated watching some tiny sand crabs, not paying attention to anything, she looked up suddenly and declared, "We'd better get out of here now. The tide rushes in awfully fast sometimes if you're not watching, and it's easy to get cut off from the rocks. You could get trapped down here with no way out easily."

At the top of the hill she led the way back down the path

to where we'd left the well-worn one to take her special one. She said, "Maybe I'll see you tomorrow," then hesitated. "That is if Aaron—what I mean is, usually Aaron and I do things together. But he's being so secretive lately," complained Olivia. "He tells me to shove off, that he wants to be by himself. I can't imagine what he finds to do all day alone, can you? I mean summers here we've always gone rock-climbing together, searched in the tide pools, gone scuba diving, fishing. I think it's very mean of him to be so exclusive, don't you?" she demanded crossly.

"Well, I enjoyed the afternoon with you immensely," I said. "I got a chance to know you a little. I hope we can do it again."

Olivia's expression shifted to a tentative smile.

"Okay, see ya!" she said, and with a toss of that beautiful coppery mane, she ran off and disappeared into the woods.

That night at dinner Justin brought up the subject of the red dress again. Nothing would do but that I go upstairs with Dortha and see it, that she try it on for me and let me see how—in his words—gorgeous she looked in it.

"It would be like one of Sargent's portraits," he mused, his eyes resting lovingly on Dortha, who looked uncomfortable.

Dortha and I went up the massive staircase together along the landing with its balcony that circled the front hall, down a short hallway to the wing where Dortha and Justin's suite was.

Dortha's room was luxurious and lovely with gray French furniture, golden velvet draperies, a satin coverlet and a golden satin puff on the bed, a cream and peach and gold thick Aubusson rug on the floor. Tiffany-style glass shades on the lamps on either side of the bed shed a mellow light, softening the room.

Once the door was closed behind us, Dortha turned to me and flung out her hands in a helpless gesture.

"What am I going to do with him, Cam? He is so

insistent about this dress. Wait until you see it. I'm sure you'll agree with me. It's not me at all, but Justin doesn't seem to realize that he sees me in an entirely unrealistic way. It's terrifying."

I could see that Dortha was working herself up. I had begun to learn her moods, her high energy that could so swiftly change to a suppressed near-hysteria. Dortha's nerves had been wearing thinner and thinner since I'd come to Gull's Glen, since we'd begun the portrait. I didn't know what secret terror she was concealing, but I felt that if Justin did not soon let up, Dortha would reach a breaking point. I can't say how I knew all this, I just felt it instinctively. Calmly I suggested she get the dress out, and I'd give her my opinion.

Dortha went over to some mirrored doors and opened them, revealing a closet filled with clothes. She seemed almost embarrassed as she said diffidently, "Justin is terribly extravagant. He buys me so many things I don't even want, can never wear. But there's no use telling him. . . ." She pushed aside several dresses on the extended rack, then brought out a plastic bag, unzipped it, and drew from it a dress of shimmering red satin. She looked at me and made a face. "I guess I'll have to try it on for you. He'll be sure and ask if I did."

Quickly she undressed, stepping out of the simple pale green sheath she'd worn at dinner. Dortha had a beautiful, gracefully slim body in her creamy lace bra and panties but when she put on the red evening gown, I saw at once it had been designed for a more statuesque, voluptuous figure. It was dramatically cut off one shoulder, gathered into folds just under the bosom with a cut-stone brooch. There was a slit up the front, and a small train in back. It was totally unsuited for Dortha's delicate beauty.

"You see," she demanded. "But try telling Justin. It isn't my style at all. He won't listen. We might as well go ahead and paint me in it. Nothing less is going to satisfy him." She sighed, and began to slip out of the dress. It dropped to the floor, lying in a silken pool at her feet as she turned to me with tears of frustration gathering in her eyes, and said despairingly, "I just wish Justin had never gotten the idea of this portrait in his head. It's like he's somehow reliving the past. As if by doing the same thing, he'll somehow—oh, I don't know. Don't pay any attention to me, Cam. I'm just edgy, that's all. I didn't mean that about the portrait. I'm glad you're here, really I am. I like you. It's just that . . . oh, forget everything I'm saying. We'll just do what Justin wants. That way everyone will be happy."

I didn't like the frantic note I detected in Dortha's voice. In spite of what she told me, it would be hard to forget what she had said.

When we went back downstairs, Bianca was sitting at a table in the bay window setting out cards, and Justin was getting out a projector.

"I thought I'd show our slides of Greece, Dortha. Don't you think Cam and Bianca would enjoy seeing them? We have some truly beautiful ones."

He brought his carousel of slides out and started adjusting the lights.

"Come on, Bianca," he urged, "I'm getting ready to project the first of the lot. I need the lights off."

"Just a minute, Justin. I'm almost through," she replied.

We all waited a few minutes while Bianca calmly went on dealing cards out from the stack she held in one hand, pausing and studying each one as she placed it down. Finally Justin, with an edge of irritation in his voice, spoke to her sharply. "For heaven's sake, Bianca, we're all waiting."

"I'll be through in just a moment, Justin." This time Bianca spoke very slowly and precisely, with exaggerated patience. But Justin would have none of it. He exploded.

"Oh, *please!* Stop making that childish fortune-telling

game so damned important. It's all utter nonsense anyhow."

I was startled, not only by Justin's anger but by the fact that Bianca was reading fortune cards. I had thought she was playing solitaire.

Bianca fixed him with a cold stare.

"That's only your opinion, Justin. I happen to know that the tarot cards often are far more accurate than any of our mere observations or opinions. As you know, they have—in the past—foretold some events accurately." But even as she was speaking, she rose and gathered up the cards, put them in a small carrying case, and came over to where Justin had arranged chairs facing the screen.

No more was said, but there was tangible tension in the room.

The slides of Greece were beautiful, and Justin's commentary was interesting and informative. However, in spite of it, I found my mind wandering. There were so many undercurrents in every conversation, in every incident, in even the most ordinary occasion among the people living at Gull's Glen. I had never experienced anything like it anywhere else. It was disturbing, even sinister.

When Justin had shown the last slide and the lights were turned on again, Bianca excused herself almost immediately. I looked at Dortha and was shocked to see how pale she was. Dark circles were shadowing her eyes which had that frightened look again.

"Well, shall we all have a brandy nightcap?" Justin was saying as he closed up the projector.

"Not for me, Justin," Dortha said. "I'm feeling suddenly very tired. I think I'll just go up to bed."

He looked at her with concern.

"You do look a little wan and weary, darling. And you must get your beauty sleep for your sitting tomorrow, so Cam and I will excuse you this time, won't we, Cam?" He kissed Dortha tenderly, then walked with her to the doorway and watched her as she went slowly up the staircase.

"I'm glad you haven't deserted me, Cam," he said jovially as he returned to the room. He poured two glasses of apricot brandy. After he had handed one to me, he went over to the door again, looked out into the hall, then closed the doors quietly and came back. He took a seat on the sofa beside me and sighed deeply.

"I'm going to be bluntly frank with you, Cam. I'm terribly worried about Dortha," he said. "She's not been herself at all, not since about a week or two after we arrived back at Gull's Glen. At first she seemed spellbound by the beauty of this place. We took long walks along the beach, went into Carmel, did the galleries, ate at all the nicest restaurants before they got crowded with the summer tourists. She seemed to be enjoying herself, having a good time. Then something happened . . . I don't know what. She began to talk about wanting to leave. This was after I'd already written you to come to start the portrait. Even when I explained I couldn't leave, that I had to get my partial to my publisher—that this was the only place I can really get a book going—I don't know. I'm discouraged. She's getting worse every day, restless, nervous." He took a sip of the brandy, stared moodily into the fire, and shook his head. "I'm at a loss. I don't know what to do."

"The portrait is going well, Justin," I said softly, hoping to give him some comfort.

"Is it really?" he asked, not waiting for an answer. "I'm planning a small dinner party this week, inviting some old friends, among them Ted Sparrow and his wife. Ted's a doctor. I want him to observe Dortha without her knowing it. She seems so upset, so nervous, as if she were on the verge of a collapse of some kind. Maybe I'm being overly concerned, but I'd like a professional opinion just the same." He frowned, and suddenly Justin looked his age, lines etched deeply on his forehead and around his mouth.

For the first time since my arrival, I saw under that

mask of joviality and self-confidence to the tension and anxiety just beneath the surface of his manner.

The silence stretched for an agonizingly long moment. I wished there were something I could say to relieve his worry, but how could I? I, too, felt there was something troubling Dortha, something no one else knew about, something she could not share with anyone.

CHAPTER 14

I was tired when I let myself into the guest cottage later, but the minute I did I was instantly aware of a difference. The feeling was vague, almost indefinable and yet real. I looked around and as I did so felt a ripple of unease. Nothing seemed out of place, but somehow I knew someone had been in there while I was up at the main house.

I moved around cautiously and still could not pinpoint the reason why I felt the way I did. It wasn't Rachel. She had come earlier in the evening with fresh towels and had turned down the bed while I was still dressing for dinner.

I sat down on the sofa and my eyes swept the room. Maybe I was letting the tension among the Bradfords get to me.

I must not allow myself to get caught up in their tangled affairs, I told myself at length. It would sap my creative energy if I got involved in whatever was going on among the various members of the family.

My job was to paint Dortha's picture, not solve other people's problems. That's what I needed to concentrate on. Wearily I got up and went into the bedroom.

I didn't even look at the portrait of Dortha as I usually did the last thing at night to get some perspective on the next day's work. I felt exhausted and hoped I could go right to sleep.

I slept heavily and woke up later than I had planned. I hurried to dress, make coffee and set up my palette for the day's painting. I was surprised to have both Dortha and Justin knock at the door precisely at ten.

I noticed right away that Justin was carrying the red dress encased in its plastic bag. He seemed in a particularly cheerful mood, although Dortha was not.

Her face was pale, her eyes had a faraway look, the mouth drooped wearily. She was looking at me but not really seeing me.

"I hope you won't mind cutting down on the posing time this morning, Cam," said Justin. "I'm kidnapping Dortha today. We're driving down the coast to a very special place I want to take her to for dinner. It's our monthly anniversary celebration and I've got some terrific plans."

I assured him that was all right with me.

"Well, I'll be back for you later, then, darling," he said to Dortha and kissed her. To me he said, "Shall I just hang this over here? Any chance I can peek at the painting?"

"I'd rather you didn't just yet," I said, not knowing how he'd react to the casually posed portrait that was nearing completion and was not, I knew, the glamorous, formal portrait he had in mind.

"All right, fine. I'll wait for the unveiling," he said. "Have a good session, you two. See you at eleven." With a wave he left.

Dortha sighed, and immediately dug into her canvas tote bag for a cigarette. "We'll have to start on the one in the dress today, Cam," she said. "There's no escaping it."

"I suppose not." I smiled at her understandingly. "After all, he is paying for the portrait, and it should be what he wants."

She nodded but made no move to change her clothes,

just sat there smoking and staring beyond me out the window with the ocean view.

I thought it best to leave her alone for a few minutes to settle down and compose herself. I went over to my work table and started selecting some brushes. I would have to start a new canvas today, if I had time. At least I'd have to make some sketches of Dortha in the red gown. I couldn't find my favorite soft-lead sketching pencils and my art gum and large sketch pad on the shelves behind the easel. Then I remembered I'd put them into the basket I'd carried to the beach the day I'd intended to sketch and paint. Now where was the basket? I remembered putting it down when I came into the cottage because I was late and in a hurry to bathe and dress for dinner. Had Rachel moved it somewhere when she was cleaning? I looked around, puzzled. Then I saw it on the lower shelf of the bookcase next to the front door and beside the fireplace. I hurried over to retrieve what I needed, only to find it was empty. What had Rachel done with the contents? It seemed unlikely that she would have removed them. Rachel was scrupulous about not touching anything I left out, even to leaving a bobby pin or a scarf just where I put it down.

"I'm ready to change and sit now, Cam," Dortha was saying.

I couldn't take any longer to try to figure out what had happened to my supplies. I would just have to make do with the pencils and drawing paper I had on hand now.

I concentrated on capturing the details of the dress and its folds on Dortha's figure. There was no use in sketching her face today, I saw at a glance. Whatever was going on inside her this morning was not what I wanted to transmit to a portrait.

"Did you know Bianca reads those damn cards nearly every night?" she broke the silence at length by asking me.

I shook my head and kept sketching.

"It's really so weird. It's like she's not getting the answers she wants from them so she keeps putting them out night after night hoping to get the right message. Whatever that is!"

Although Dortha's tone was slightly sarcastic, I felt that underneath it was tinged with fear.

"Bianca is terribly superstitious, believes in all sorts of signs and symbols, had her horoscope charted by someone in San Francisco, had the children's done, too. Justin was furious about it. He pretends he thinks it all just silly, but I believe he hates Bianca's doing things like that. It makes him very uneasy."

"Well, a lot of people are into astrology," I commented, trying to keep the conversation neutral, not wanting to be drawn into discussing Bianca in a negative way.

"I think Bianca enjoys seeing Justin disturbed," Dortha went on. "She must know how it throws off his ability to concentrate on his work. She'll make some chance remark intentionally designed to upset him. It's like she has some kind of power over him she delights in using. Anything about the children will set him off. Whatever he doesn't want them to do, she'll somehow support them for doing."

I didn't answer. Dortha seemed to be talking more to herself than to me anyway. Maybe she needed to get some of this off her chest. Maybe Dortha couldn't openly confront Bianca about the things she felt were bothering Justin. At least she could vent some of her feelings safely here with me. I went on sketching. I was having difficulty getting her left hand, the one that seemed weighted down with the large emerald. Finally, in exasperation, I sketched in a fold of the dress to cover it.

Suddenly Dortha stood up. I looked at her. She was trembling, almost shivering. Again I saw that stricken look on her face.

"You know what all this is, don't you? Justin's insisting on coming back here, having my portrait painted—this whole thing is superstition on his part, whether he'll admit it or not. It's an exercise in exorcism for him. Get rid of the ghost of Rosalind! But it's dreadful . . . and I don't want any part in it!"

She started walking to where she had placed her clothes, undoing the zipper of the red satin gown as she moved, tearing at it with feverishly eager fingers.

"I can't sit anymore today, Cam. I'm sorry, but I just can't."

She dragged off the dress, flung it across a chair, got into her pants and top in minutes, grabbed up her sweater and tote bag and half-ran out of the cottage door, letting it slam behind her.

I watched her out the window, saw that instead of taking the wooded path to the house, she turned in the direction of the beach.

There was nothing more I could do today either. I put away what I'd done, little as it was, and decided that whatever had happened to my supplies, they'd have to be replaced. Taking off my painting smock, I got my car keys and drove to Carmel.

Jeff was busy with another customer, but he smiled and signaled he'd be with me in a minute. I took the opportunity to go into the gallery and look at the paintings. There were several seascapes by different artists, the popular kind of painting bought by tourists. I was particularly drawn to some colorful still lifes done in bright acrylics. They were semirealistic renderings of ordinary household objects—pottery, kitchen utensils, fruits and vegetables, and flowers, seashells, garden tools and potted plants—the things one would ordinarily find around the house, but never appreciate or paint. They were charming, and I looked closer to read the artist's signature.

"They're Nell Sparrow's," a voice behind me said.

I turned and saw Jeff had come into the gallery.

"Sparrow? Why does that sound familiar?" I wondered out loud.

"She's a local artist, but you may have seen her prints in the Bay Area. She does a limited number of prints from some of her paintings, and they're sold in gift shops as posters and notepaper," he explained.

I frowned, accepting his explanation, but thinking the name had some other connection. Then I remembered. Justin had said his doctor friend's name was Sparrow, Ted Sparrow. I wondered if this Nell Sparrow was some relation. I didn't bother to pursue this with Jeff; instead I brought out my list.

"You really go through this stuff, don't you?" Jeff grinned as he began to gather together my pencils, sketch pads, and drawing pens. "You just bought these same items the other day, didn't you? Not that I'm objecting. Good business. Besides, I was wondering how to get in touch with you. The Bradfords have an unlisted number, naturally, so I just had to hope you'd come in again. My lucky day, I guess." He was wrapping my supplies into a neat package. "I wanted to ask you if you'd have dinner with me some night. Tonight, specifically. I have tickets for the Studio-Theatre Restaurant. It's a local group with a sprinkling of professionals. They're doing *The Philadelphia Story* currently. They serve dinner at seven, curtain's at eight thirty. It's a lot of fun, and they're really quite good. Would you like to go?"

I was surprised by my own delighted response. Jeff was the first man to whom I'd reacted with more than mild interest for a long time. Since Doug, as a matter of fact. I had just assumed that someone as attractive as Jeff would already have something going. My surprise prompted a quick answer.

"Why, yes, that sounds like fun. I'd like to," I said.

He seemed pleased.

"Great! What time shall I pick you up?" he asked, all smiles.

"It's a long way out to Gull's Glen, so why don't I just meet you?"

He raised his eyebrows. "I don't mind."

"Oh, I'm sure you don't, but I'd rather."

I always liked to be independent on a first date, and usually made it a point to have my own transportation. Of course, I was a bit out of practice dating. For the last three years it had been just Doug.

"You're sure?" he asked quizzically.

"Yes, quite sure."

"Then how about here? I close up at five, and my place is on the street, just in back. We can walk to the Studio-Theatre from here easily."

I stopped at the house on my way back to the cottage to tell Bianca I would be out for dinner that evening. Just as I pulled up out front, she was coming down the terrace steps. When I told her, she said she was on her way down to my cottage to tell me that since Justin and Dortha were going to be out, she would send a tray down for my supper.

"But now I'll tell Rachel it won't be necessary. I'm glad you're going to have an evening out with friends. I'm going down to Rosalind's cottage now, so perhaps I'll just ride along with you, if I may?"

"Of course." I held open the car door.

She got in and I started down the narrow road that led to the site of the three guest cottages. I wondered what she meant by Rosalind's cottage. Was that the shrine Dortha had told me about?

Bianca brought my mind back sharply to the present as she said, "Cameron? Isn't that an odd name for a girl?" Immediately she said, "Sorry, that was terribly rude of me, especially for someone who has a name like mine. But there's always an explanation for names, isn't there? Of course there was in our case . . . Rosalind's and mine. Our father was a Shakespeare buff, as they say. And 'What's in a name?' anyhow, as the Bard himself would ask—'a rose by any other name . . .' Somehow, though, Rosalind really suited—" Here Bianca broke off abruptly, a shadow passing over her expressive face.

"Well, in my case, it's a family name," I said, "and,

whether it was a boy or a girl, my parents had decided to use it. It's helpful sometimes in signing my paintings. You might not believe it, but some gallery owners have a prejudice against women painters."

"Why do you suppose that is?" Bianca frowned.

I shrugged. "Perhaps they feel they're not serious artists. You know, only a few women artists have made it to the top ranks of art, although I believe it's beginning to open up more nowadays."

"The theater, I think, is the exact opposite. There have been more renowned actresses than actors. You can almost count the male stars of the theater on one hand—I mean the really great ones—but women . . . well, just think. Sarah Bernhardt, Eleanora Duse, Mrs. Patrick Campbell, Ellen Terry, Mrs. Sarah Siddons, Helen Hayes, Ethel Barrymore, Katherine Cornell, on and on . . ."

As I'd noticed before when Bianca talked of the theater, actors, or acting, her whole expression changed. Instead of the cool, composed mask she usually wore, her face became animated, alive.

We'd come to the clearing in the woods where the little group of cottages were and I stopped the car. Unexpectedly Bianca asked, "Would you like to come in and see Rosalind's things? I have all her costumes from her different roles and her scrapbook of clippings. She got some marvelous reviews. Pictures and photographs, Hollywood stills taken when she was under contract to one of the major studios—I've kept everything—"

"Why, yes, I'd love to see them," I answered, really surprised that she had invited me.

As I followed her to the third cottage, I felt excited. After hearing about Rosalind, I was going to get a chance to see what she looked like, get a glimpse of the person she was, the one everyone seemed to have a different impression of. Yes, I was eager to see it all.

Bianca opened the door and led the way inside. I found

myself walking softly as though I actually was entering some kind of shrine.

The interior of the cottage was very like the one I was using, except that most of the furnishings had been removed. Instead there were several tableaux—the only way I can describe them. They were small stage settings, each with a backdrop depicting a play in which Rosalind had evidently appeared—the balcony scene from *Romeo and Juliet* was one. On a dress form was a white velvet gown with a damask panel, long pointed sleeves, and a square neckline trimmed in tiny pearls. On a draped table beside it was the famous jeweled Juliet cap and the dagger from the death scene. There were other sets for her roles as Ophelia in *Hamlet,* and as Cordelia in *King Lear,* all dramatically presented.

Bianca was watching my reaction.

"It's fantastic!" I murmured. "Really amazing," was all I could muster. Inwardly I thought it was actually rather morbid.

As if echoing my thoughts, Bianca said with a trace of bitterness, "Justin doesn't approve of my doing this. But of course he hated Rosalind's acting, her preoccupation with the theater. He made her give it up when she married him, you know. The children are really too young to fully appreciate what I'm doing or to realize what a great actress their mother could have been if her career had not been cut off before it peaked."

She walked over to one of the costumes, and touched it caressingly. Her long slender hands moved carefully, lovingly over the velvet folds, tracing the silver and gold embroidery, the braid trimmed with tiny pearls.

"Some day Aaron and Olivia will know and be grateful that I've preserved all this for them. It may be all they have after all."

Bianca's face hardened. "You know, Gull's Glen was really Rosalind's," she continued. "She bought it with the enormous salary the studio paid her, even though they never gave her a part worthy of her talents. Of course, at her death, it became Justin's. She left everything to him in her will. She assumed he would take care of her children." Here Bianca's voice roughened. "But now he's changed *his* will to include Dortha, so I don't know what the children will inherit now." She paused, then went on. "At least they'll have this. No one can take the heritage their mother left them. Her beauty was extraordinary. Her potential was so great . . ." Bianca's voice died out. She shook her head regretfully. She motioned with her hand to the shelves of bulging scrapbooks.

"Some day when you have time you might want to look through those. I have pictures of every play Rosalind was ever in—the playbills, the reviews, letters from the casts after the show closed. Just ask me for the key if you should want to spend an hour or so."

Outside, the day was darkening. All at once a chill quivered through my body. I felt I wanted to get out of there into what sunlight was left of the day. I felt a sense of cloying depression in this room surrounded by all the artifacts of a dead woman.

I said something about having to go and get ready for my evening. Bianca nodded absentmindedly. She was already poring over a large volume spread out on the work table at the back of the room, and did not even seem to notice as I left. For some reason, I couldn't explain why, I tiptoed out.

CHAPTER 15

As I was getting ready that evening for my date with Jeff, I suddenly realized how much I was looking forward to it. It wasn't like all the times that past spring when I'd made myself accept invitations, dragged myself out, trying to convince myself that even a boring escort was better than sitting home alone thinking about Doug. Tonight I actually felt a tingle of excitement.

This must be some kind of milestone, I told myself. And because I really felt it was, I wanted to look very special.

After trying on three different outfits, I finally decided on a blue boucle knit. Putting on turquoise earrings in front of the mirror, I noticed with some satisfaction that I looked better than I had in months. The color of the dress did nice things for my eyes. There was an apricot tone to my skin, tanned now from my daily walks on the beach, and new golden streaks in my short brown hair.

Taking so much time to dress ran me a little late, and Jeff was out in front of the store waiting for me when I pulled up.

"Sorry, I'm late," I said, somewhat breathless.

"It's okay, you were worth waiting for." He grinned, his eyes sweeping over me with more than casual admiration.

He looked very handsome himself in a beige hopsacking sports jacket, blue Oxford cloth shirt with a cotton patchwork tie, and brown slacks.

The theater restaurant was only a few short blocks from the framing shop and as we walked over, I had the feeling it was going to be a wonderful evening.

It was. Right from the beginning Jeff made me feel comfortable and at ease and very happy I'd come.

Evidently Jeff was well known in Carmel, because as we were shown to our reserved table, many people greeted him. Our table was near the stage and so we had fine seats for the play after dinner.

We had a choice of entree, chicken or steak, and we both opted for steak. While we waited for our order, Jeff explained, "They're not allowed to sell alcoholic beverages inside the theater, so perhaps you'd like to go for a drink after the performance. I would have suggested cocktails beforehand, but I know the curtain goes up promptly at eight thirty and I wanted us to have time for a leisurely dinner, to get better acquainted."

"That's fine. Frankly I'm starved anyway," I answered. "I should warn you, my appetite has increased enormously since I've been here! The sea air, or something."

"Well, whatever it is, it's very becoming," Jeff said. "So, how goes the portrait?"

I hesitated. I didn't want to unburden all my troubles with the painting on him, although I had a hunch Jeff would be an easy person to talk to, as well as understanding. Neither did I want to lie.

"Portraits are often difficult," I began. "They're not like a still life that you can set up which will stay just the way you arrange it until you finish painting it. Portraits are—people," I laughed. "And people are unpredictable."

"I suppose even if your subject is as beautiful as the new Mrs. Bradford, there are all sorts of unforeseen problems."

"Then you know Dortha?" I asked.

"No, not really. I saw her in Carmel a couple of times, that's all. The first time was with Justin—that's how I knew it must be his new wife—then a few other times since. She drives a white Jaguar, doesn't she?"

"I don't know," I replied.

Just then the young waiter brought us our salads.

When the waiter left, I asked Jeff, "I take it you did know the first Mrs. Bradford—Rosalind?"

"Yes. Not well, but once you'd met her—well, Rosalind Bradford was not someone you were likely to forget."

"Tell me your impression. I've just been talking with her sister, Bianca, who made her sound more like a myth than a real woman. Talented, exciting, beautiful—"

"I guess you could say she was all those things. Beautiful? I wouldn't have called Rosalind beautiful—attractive, dramatic looking, a bit too theatrical in appearance for my taste." Jeff paused. "I liked her, though. She seemed to be involved in everything. She was real independent. Rode a little Honda motorbike all around. Whatever was going on locally, she was part of it. My first meeting with her was right after I'd bought the store. She came in, saying how glad she was that someone had taken over, was doing new things. There hadn't been a gallery in here before, and I started showing unknown artists' work. Then she wanted to enlist me with some of the other merchants she was contacting to sponsor a Shakespeare week here. That was one of her pet projects. It never really got off the ground, although they had quite a few meetings about it. She had a drama school provide apprentices to work on sets, scenery, and for minor roles in return for the experience and room and board. Rosalind was real enthusiastic about it . . . but then she died."

The voices and laughter around us gradually increased, raising the noise level in the small room. By the time our dinners arrived, conversation was nearly impossible. We smiled at each other, shrugged, and ate heartily. When our waiter brought our coffee, it was almost time for the curtain. An anticipatory hush fell over the crowd as the tables were removed, and everyone shifted their chairs to face the stage. There followed a rustle of program consulting, then the house lights dimmed and in a few minutes the curtains swung open for the first act.

The play was light and funny and extremely well done for an amateur group. Afterward Jeff and I walked along the cobblestone sidewalk to the small bistro he'd mentioned. We went down stone steps to a patio overhung with trees. At redwood burl slab tables, we ordered Kahlúa. We talked of the play and then Jeff mentioned Aaron, and my ears perked up.

"He's been in the gallery a couple of times lately. I just wondered if he was interested in art."

"I don't know," I answered slowly. "He's been banished from the dinner hour for surly behavior, I guess you'd call it. I haven't seen him around for days."

"He didn't buy anything, but I saw him looking at brushes and tubes of paint," Jeff commented. "I know what you mean about surly. I asked him if he needed any help, and he just scowled and walked out."

That was all we said about Aaron, but for some reason the thought of him lingered in my mind. A strange troubled boy—what was it Olivia had said, that he had been slipping away by himself lately?

"Are you sure you don't want me to follow you home in my car?" Jeff asked, as we stood in front of my VW an hour later.

"Oh, no, I'll be fine. Besides, look at the moon. It's going to be like driving in daylight," I said, getting out my keys.

He held out his hand for them, unlocked and opened the car door for me. I got in. He closed the door and then leaned in the window I unrolled.

"You're sure?" he asked again.

"Positive. And thanks, Jeff, for a marvelous evening. I really had a great time."

He handed me my keys. "Me, too. We'll do it again."

"Good night, and thanks again," I said, starting the engine.

"Good night, Cam." He reached in the car window, turned my face to him, then lightly kissed me. "I don't know when I've enjoyed being with anyone as much."

Driving back to Gull's Glen, I couldn't believe how happy I felt. It had been months since I'd felt so free and lighthearted. It was as if, within hours, all the hurt, humiliation, and self-doubt that Doug's rejection had caused had simply disappeared. Jeff's open and obvious interest in me surely was partly responsible. The whole evening contrasted sharply with the kind Doug and I used to have. Jeff seemed genuinely interested in my work and in me as a person, totally different from Doug's self-centered absorption in his own career.

I hadn't ever met anyone as sure of himself as Jeff

seemed to be without being arrogant or conceited. He knew who he was, liked what he was doing, knew what he wanted out of life. He was completely at ease with himself, so he could reach out to others.

I pulled up in front of the cottage and sat for a moment leaning on the steering wheel, entranced by the beauty of the night. Even the denseness of the surrounding trees had not completely obscured the moon, and as I watched, a cloud parted and a shaft of moonlight filtered down, totally blanketing everything in a luminous glow. It was a night filled with romance, the air tinged with a special sweetness, the atmosphere imbued with magic. It was a night for lovers.

I sighed and abruptly got out of the car and went into the cottage.

"Don't get carried away," I warned myself out loud. "Sure Jeff is attractive and charming, but remember what you promised yourself about not getting involved again."

I got ready for bed and stretched out. I still felt stimulated by the evening I'd just spent. I kept going over our conversation. The brief mention of Rosalind Bradford stayed with me, too. It seemed each person who knew her had a different impression of the woman. Jeff's had been a more casual observation than any of the others except Ennis Shelby's. But the personality of the first Mrs. Bradford intrigued me. Evidently she had made a lasting effect on everyone.

Thinking of Rosalind naturally brought to mind Dortha. It seemed Justin had chosen a very different kind of woman for his second wife. Where Rosalind had been outgoing, Dortha was shy. While Rosalind loved being center stage, Dortha remained in shadow. Rosalind was fearless, while Dortha seemed to live on the knife's edge of fear.

Thinking of Dortha, my mind became wide awake. What was going on with her? Why could she not shrug off the natural reluctance of Justin's children to accept a stepmother, especially when abetted by their hostile aunt, the resentful sister of the dead woman? In a few years Aaron and Olivia both would be out on their own. Even now, they were away at school nine months of the year. It would only be a matter of time until she and Justin could live their own lives freely. Why, when her husband obviously adored her, was Dortha so insecure?

All these unanswered questions swirled fitfully in my brain until I sat up in bed totally awake. I felt uneasy, restless. I knew it would be impossible to go to sleep, not with the moon making the room almost as bright as day. I got out of bed, went over to the window, and looked out. The moon shed a silver path across the ocean. It was so exquisite I was lost for a few moments in simply absorbing it. The night wind was gentle, and as I stood there, all at once I wanted to be outside, drenching myself in this unusual beauty.

Quickly I slipped on jeans, pulled on a sweater, and jammed my feet into sandals. I walked through the living room, pushed back the latch of the front door, opened it, and stepped out into the moonlight.

It was a fairyland, everything touched with a silvery sheen. I walked along the path leading to the ocean, a feeling of excitement brought on by the exquisite beauty of the night. *If only there were someone to share it with,* I thought wistfully.

I took the secret path Olivia had shown me and soon emerged at the crest of the knoll. I sat on the bench in the small, sheltered enclosure from where I had a sweeping view of the ocean. Breathless with awe at the beauty of the moonlight on the water, I watched transfixed. Wave after wave rolled onto the beach, scattering phosphorescent sprays like handfuls of glittering sequins.

I don't know how long I was there absorbing the beautiful scene. It must have been quite a while because it was with some feeling of intrusion that I was snapped out of my solitary enjoyment. I became aware of two figures walking together along the edge of the ocean. Every so often they would stop as if in an animated conversation, oblivious to the magic of this night. Then they continued on down the beach and out of my sight.

I thought it was probably Justin and Dortha. Returning from their anniversary dinner, they had noticed the moon and decided to take a romantic moonlight walk.

Suddenly I felt lonely. A wave of longing to be with someone I loved who loved me swept over me. I yearned with a newly awakened need to belong to someone who cared deeply for me. I knew that that was what I wanted deep down— Beyond goals or career or success, I needed the ultimate fulfillment of loving and being loved in return.

CHAPTER 16

The next morning by ten thirty, Dortha still had not arrived for her sitting. I was beginning to wonder about it when a tap came at the cottage door and before I could go to open it, Olivia stuck her head inside.

"My father says to tell you Dortha won't be coming this morning. She isn't feeling well. So can we go to the beach? Want to take a picnic?"

My immediate reaction was skepticism. What was the real reason behind the flimsy excuse that Dortha wasn't coming? Of course, I didn't give my feelings away to Olivia. Instead I said enthusiastically, "That's a great idea. Let's see what we can find in the refrigerator."

"I could go back up to the house and see if Rachel will pack up some sandwiches," Olivia began rather reluctantly. "But Cook always gets so cross when Aaron and I ask, we usually just snitch something. Then she gets really mad and then Aunt Bianca finds out . . . and it's too much of a hassle."

"Oh, I think we can scrounge up enough for the two of us," I said.

We found cheese, crackers, a couple of small cans of juice, some pears and grapes. We put these in my basket, grabbed a blanket, and were off.

Outside the cottage the two Weimaraners waited.

"You don't mind if I bring the dogs, do you?" she asked. "Aaron has really neglected them lately. He goes off somewhere by himself, and they need the exercise. Dad's locked up in his study, working, and Dortha . . . well, Dortha is afraid of them." This last was said scornfully.

"Well, some people aren't used to dogs, and being around them frightens them. Bruno and Clovis are awfully big. I can see how someone could be afraid of them."

Olivia looked me squarely in the eyes. "Do you like Dortha?" she asked.

"Yes, very much."

"I don't."

"You would if you'd give yourself a chance to know her. She's a very sweet person," I said firmly.

Olivia gave me another glance. I could see some uncertainty in her.

"Your father loves Dortha. It would be nice if you could learn to like her and accept her, just because he wants that so much."

Her lower lip pushed out, she gave her head a little shake.

"You want your father to be happy, don't you?" I asked her.

The small elfin face twisted into a grimace. "I guess so," she said slowly. "Well, yes, but Aaron, he says it was disloyal of Daddy to marry Dortha . . . that they ought not to be happy."

"But that's a dreadful thing to say about anyone. I hope Aaron doesn't really feel that way."

"He does, though. He's angry at Aunt Bianca, too. He says—"

But I wasn't to learn just then why Aaron was angry at his aunt. We were down the cliffs now and starting to walk along the sand to the cove which had become our special place. The dogs had nimbly traversed the steep rocky path and now bounded into the surf, barking and leaping, tearing back along the beach, chasing the shorebirds and running after the swooping sea gulls. Then as I glanced down the beach I saw a familiar figure approaching. Ennis Shelby.

Olivia had waded into the surf and was shouting and throwing sticks for the dogs to fetch. When Ennis reached me and we exchanged greetings, she turned and came running up toward us. Then a curious thing happened. A change came over Ennis's face, a look of surprised recognition that altered his expression as Olivia joined us. He seemed to be struggling to recover himself and said something almost under his breath. As I heard it, I thought it very strange indeed.

" 'Thou art thy mother's glass and she in thee, Calls back the lovely April of her prime.' "

I didn't have time to try to figure it out or understand it, for Ennis immediately became his suave, confident self.

"I haven't seen you since you were a small girl, Olivia," he said. "Years ago. You've just reminded me of the old cliché . . . how time flies." He smiled briefly, then turned to me. "I hope you haven't forgotten we're going to set a date for dinner. I just got back and have some things I have to get caught up on, but I'll get in touch soon."

I said that would be fine, and he walked on.

The rest of the day was spent happily with Olivia. I was getting to know her better and becoming very fond of her. More and more I realized that under the surface indifference, she was a lonely little girl.

As we were coming up from the beach, we met Justin just starting down. "Got my daily stint at the typewriter done," he said, "so now I'm going to try to clear my brain with a brisk walk and some sea air." I felt he was making an attempt at a heartiness he didn't feel.

"I hope Dortha's better," I said.

His heavy brows came together in a frown. "She's been in bed most of the day, although I think she's beginning to feel better now. It was the strangest thing. Everything was going beautifully. Last night we had just ordered dinner, been served our wine, when suddenly Dortha got deathly pale, said she felt faint. She excused herself but was gone such a long time I got worried. I waited for her outside the ladies' room. Eventually I asked a lady coming out if anyone fitting Dortha's description was in there, ill. She checked but said there was no one in there at all. In a few minutes Dortha came through the entrance from the parking lot, explaining she felt she needed some fresh air. But she asked to be taken home. So, we came straight home, and Dortha went right to bed. It was a sorry end to what was to have been a delightful evening."

I hoped I made a sympathetic reply. I don't remember what I said because all the time my mind was demanding an answer to the question: "If not Dortha and Justin on the moonlight beach last night . . . then *who*?"

CHAPTER 17

The next morning as I sat drinking my first cup of coffee, wondering vaguely if Dortha would show up for today's sitting, I found my thoughts centering on Jeff. Was it possible that after only a few meetings I could be falling in love? It could be that I was on the brink of a rebound romance, so eager to be loved again that I was imagining not only my own interest, but Jeff's as well. He was much too nice a person to use. I'd have to be careful, I told myself.

That may have been why I decided to accept the invitation to dinner from Ennis Shelby that Rachel brought me later. She said it had been delivered that morning.

The message, written on a memo pad with his name and a San Francisco address at the top, was scribbled in a haphazard slant. It read: "How about dinner tonight? If yes, I'll be at the bottom of the beach steps at six to meet you. Sunset at 6:40 tonight. Hope you can make it."

Rachel had been replenishing my towel supply, and restocking the tiny refrigerator with juice and milk as I read the note.

"Is Mrs. Bradford up this morning, Rachel?" I asked.

"Not yet, miss. I took a tray to her room. She just wanted tea."

"Then she still isn't feeling well?"

"I don't think so, miss. She asked me not to open the drapes and wanted me to bring her some aspirin from the bathroom."

Another day with no work on the portrait, I sighed.

Well, that was that. There was certainly nothing I could do about it. I could not insist on Dortha's sitting and the portrait was at a point that I could not go on without her.

Since I still had not explored Carmel to my own satisfaction, I decided I might as well drive in and do some more brousing. I would also accept Ennis Shelby's dinner invitation.

Carmel-by-the-Sea! Even the name has a magic, I thought, as I turned in from the highway and drove slowly into the center of town. I had heard about Carmel for years. In fact, Aunt Mim had mentioned that she and Uncle Ted had gone there on their honeymoon, calling it an enchanted place. I had wondered if it somehow would fall short of what must have been a description of her romance-wrapped memory of it. But as I nosed my little car into a narrow parking space on one of the side streets and looked around me, I thought, maybe not. Even on this block away from the main thoroughfare, I saw two or three interesting-looking shops.

It was lucky that the building right in front of where I parked was a gallery with a large, impressive seascape in its window because otherwise I might never have found my car again. As I started down the cobblestone sidewalk, one after another irresistible place beckoned. The buildings formed a labyrinth of courts, one leading into the other, seemingly endless, each with its own unique attraction. And on all sides were flowers. The color on this sunlit morning was dazzling—flower boxes and planters stood on every side, with vivid blue trailing lobelia, cheerful orange, gold and red nasturtiums, interspersed with white alyssum and yellow daisies, petunias in all shades of pink to purple, begonias in hanging baskets. In addition, bright geraniums brightened window boxes outside the many little shops hidden away in the inner courts.

I wandered in and out from one shop to the other, dazed by the profusion of beautiful gifts and merchandise available—paintings, handcrafts, jewelry, imported clothing, pottery, and toys.

I found gifts for everyone I thought of: scented candles uniquely sculptured into miniature sand castles for my twin cousins; a lovely antique silver and lavender enameled pillbox for Aunt Mim; a charming stained glass medallion to hang in a window for my mother. From the Hermitage Shop I ordered one of the famous monk's fruitcakes to be mailed at Christmas to my grandparents back east.

At last I began to feel hungry and noticed it was after noon. There were so many enticing restaurants, tearooms and coffeeshops, I did not know which one to choose. I was standing outside the window of Scandia reading the posted luncheon menu, when a voice behind me asked, "Could I interest you in a guided tour, miss?"

Automatically I looked up and saw Jeff Maxwell's reflection beside mine in the window. I turned around and he was grinning down at me.

"You're the last person I expected to see today!" he said. "I thought you'd be slaving away over a hot easel."

I sighed. "Sitting postponed—again! Dortha wasn't feeling well. But at least it gave me a chance to come here and play tourist. This is an incredible place!"

"I know. It's great, isn't it? At the risk of sounding smug, what else could you ask for in a place to live and work?"

"Speaking of work—who's minding the store?" I teased.

"This is my lunch break. I just put a sign on the door from noon until two or so." Again came that grin that brought a boyish, mischievous look into Jeff's face.

"Have you been to the Plaza shops yet?" he asked.

I threw up my hands in mock astonishment. "You mean there are more! I thought I'd just about done them all."

"Not by a half. Then there's The Barnyard. You haven't been down there yet, have you?"

I shook my head. "If my feet lasted, I'm not sure my pocketbook would!" I exclaimed. "I've already bought gifts for several people and now there's more temptation on the way."

"Let me misquote: 'Eye hath not seen, nor beheld—the glories that await.' I don't know what that's from, but I mean to show you." Jeff grinned, and tucked my arm through his after taking some of my bundles. "Now, I'll tell you what we're going to do. First we'll stow these at my shop, then—"

"Then what?" I asked laughingly.

"Then, we're going to play hooky."

At his shop he put all my packages behind the counter,

then he put a sign on the door, SORRY! CLOSED! locked it and said, "Come on."

If we had planned it we couldn't have picked a more perfect day to run away. It was sunny and bright, with a soft wind from the sea. As we drove south in Jeff's TR-6 with the top down, the fog seemed to disappear, and I really did feel as free and fun-seeking as any schoolgirl on an unexpected holiday.

We stopped first at The Barnyard, an intriguing cluster of authentic barns which housed another varied group of shops. As we strolled the brick walkways, and took a stairway which led to another new cluster of shops, galleries, and antique shops, I remarked to Jeff, "Does this bore you? I mean, it's rather like a busman's holiday for you, isn't it?"

"No, actually I don't get to do this sort of thing in Carmel. Too busy minding the store." He smiled.

We wandered in and out of each shop that interested either of us. Leather goods and pottery and pewter were especially fascinating to both of us. Then, in the Thunderbird Bookstore, we both got lost for a good half hour and each ended up buying several books. We had bowls of steaming clam chowder in the attractive restaurant connected to it, then did more window-shopping. The Oriental jewelry shop took another half hour as I marveled at the lovely jade and pearls, and the Scotch Shop, where I looked up the Cameron tartan and bought an authentic clan plaid tie for my father, took an hour. We found a shady bench to stop and rest on while we ate double-dip cones Jeff got us at The Creamery, and tried to decide what to do next.

"You're not in a hurry to get back, are you?" he asked.

"No. I left a note saying I'd be gone for the day, so I'm sure they're not expecting me back any certain time," I replied, as I focused on not letting any of the delicious mocha fudge drip down my hand.

"Then I think we should definitely drive down to Monterey and have dinner on Cannery Row," Jeff said.

"You mean *the* Cannery Row of John Steinbeck fame?"

"The very same . . . although, to be truthful, it's been prettied up a bit for the tourists," Jeff admitted. "As I understand it, a strange phenomenon happened about 1945," Jeff added. "The pilchard, which is a small silver sardine, used to flourish in Monterey Bay. Fishermen caught them by the millions and prospered. A whole industry was built on this tiny fish. There really used to be canning factories all along what you'll see is now another tourist mecca of shops, galleries, and the like. Then suddenly, as if by a silent vote, the pilchards decided that if they stayed in Monterey Bay they'd all eventually end up between two slices of rye bread with mustard and pickles, and they simply disappeared."

"You're kidding!"

"No, it's absolute fact. Gradually the canneries had to close, the fishermen had to go elsewhere. But, as you'll see, Cannery Row has put on a new face and built a whole new business for Monterey."

"It sounds fascinating, and I'd love to go, but I'll have to take a raincheck, Jeff."

Jeff looked disappointed. "Maybe, I'm pushing? Too much of a good thing?"

"Oh, no, it's not that. I've had a marvelous time today, it's just that I already made plans for this evening and I'll have to get back. Ennis Shelby asked me to dinner at his shack, as he calls it. He wants to show me some photographs." I stopped and asked, "Does that sound too terribly cliché? What I mean is, he has the photographs of Rosalind Bradford that Cole Bernham used in painting her portrait. He thought it would be interesting for me to see how another artist worked."

Jeff frowned, then asked, "Well, can I count on another evening? Soon?"

"Oh, yes." I smiled, meaning it.

Jeff didn't say much driving back to Carmel. Then when he walked me to where I'd parked my car, I knew he had something on his mind but didn't know exactly how to say it. He opened the car door for me, and before I got in, he touched my arm.

"Cam," he said, "maybe it's none of my business, and—maybe whatever I say could be construed as being self-serving, because obviously I have something at stake." He paused a long moment. "But for what it's worth, I feel it's only right to warn you. Ennis Shelby has quite a reputation for—no, I won't say any more. He's an interesting fellow . . . and a fine photographer." He paused, leaving me curious but respecting him for not continuing.

We stood there for a long moment looking at each other. I'm not sure which of us moved first, but the next thing I knew I was in Jeff's arms and he was kissing me, a long, sweet, very thorough kiss.

I was breathless when we slowly drew apart.

"You're really quite special, Cam, did you know that?" Jeff said quietly. Then, "Tomorrow night?"

Dazed by both the kiss and the feelings in me it had aroused, I started to say yes when I remembered Justin's dinner party. Regretfully I told Jeff about it.

"Then the next night, for sure?"

"For sure," I said.

He kissed me lightly on the lips, and we said good-bye. As I drove back to Gull's Glen, I found myself so preoccupied with thinking about him that I almost missed the sign to the Bradfords' private road.

CHAPTER 18

After Jeff's subtle warning I could not help having a few qualms as I descended the wobbly beach steps that evening a few minutes before six.

Ennis Shelby both attracted and intimidated me. It would be interesting to see what he was really like and, as usual, my curiosity about people overcame my reservations.

A little while later, sitting on the sofa in front of the open fire in Ennis Shelby's living room, sipping a glass of chilled wine and listening to Bartok on the stereo, I thought, *This is just like the setting for one of those old romantic movies on TV*. But I was not sure of my role or my lines.

Ennis brought in a tray of canapes—stuffed mushrooms, celery and carrot strips, olives, and almonds.

"So, you—as they say—did Carmel today? Gad! I hope they don't ruin it in the next few years. I avoid going downtown as much as possible during the peak summer months. Those buses disgorging all those polyester-suited tourists, jostling each other, cramming the sidewalks, jaywalking the streets. Deliver me!" He gave a sarcastic laugh.

"You begrudge them a taste of what you enjoy all the time?" I asked, half-teasing, half-serious.

"Oh, let's not analyze my motivations. Just leave it that I don't like crowds of any kind." He smiled at me indulgently.

"I am glad you enjoyed your day," he continued. "It *is* a haven for artists. I'm sure you went to the Carmel Art Association Gallery? And Ansel Adams? Of course, that's my particular favorite. He was the one made me know early on what I wanted to do." He got up. "I promised to show you some of the photographs I took of Rosalind Bradford, didn't I?" He went over to a built-in bookcase, the lower part of which had slots high enough for large, matted photographs to slip in and out easily.

"Cole—Cole Burnham, the artist who was doing her portrait—had some difficulties, mainly, I think, due to his emotional involvement with her during the sittings. But he would study my photographs for hours."

I don't know what I expected exactly, but having heard so much about Rosalind Bradford's beauty, I suppose I was anticipating a classically beautiful woman. She wasn't, at least in my opinion, nearly as beautiful as Dortha.

Ennis picked up immediately on my reaction. "She's not what you thought she'd be," he said. It was a statement, not a question.

"I guess, well, from what Bianca said, I did think she would be more—well, spectacularly beautiful."

"Rosalind was beautiful, but she seemed totally unconcerned about it, which is very unusual, especially for an actress. It was her inner beauty that attracted people. She seemed to shine somehow. Everything about her glowed. Her movements were full of eagerness and light.

"I don't think she was conscious of trying to attract—I never saw her flirt or make any effort toward any man. It was just something about her that drew people to her. I think James M. Barrie said it better than anyone when he described charm. A woman either has it or she doesn't. And if she doesn't have it, it doesn't matter much what else she has."

I glanced at Ennis. There was something in his voice when he spoke of Rosalind that puzzled me. He had seemed such an aloof man, an observer of life more than a participator, yet his tone softened to take on that hushed quality I'd noticed when Bianca had talked about her sister. I looked back at the set of photographs Ennis was propping against the wall. Rosalind—the broad, smooth brow, the strong features, the deep-set eyes, the wide mouth. If not skillfully, expertly—lovingly?—lighted, would not her face be quite ordinary? Anyone seen through the eyes of love is enhanced. A portrait artist like myself looks for the bone structure, the planes, the shape. I took another sidelong glance at Ennis. He was staring at the photographs, apparently lost in thought. Ennis was known for his scenics, his thoughtful, even poetic studies of sunlight through trees, the wild dance of waves caught at the crest, craggy rocks, the delicate design and patterns of leaves and wild flowers. There was a special field for portrait photography and this specialty was not his. To me the photographs were the result of an emotional viewpoint, not a professional one.

"What a fantastic lady," he said, almost to himself. Then, turning to me, he added, "And what a damnable waste."

"Her death, you mean?"

"Yes. Hers and Cole's, for that matter, too."

"The artist, Cole Burnham? How did he die?"

Ennis settled himself on the couch and took a sip of his wine before replying. "After the inquest—you did know there was an inquest when Cole went to the grand jury and demanded one? Of course, this intensified the furious hostility between him and Justin. The finger pointed squarely at Justin—the irrefutable motive, jealousy. Any number of people in this town could testify to incidents when they saw examples of Justin's unbridled jealousy of Rosalind. It was common knowledge."

"You blame Justin for her death—" I asked haltingly.

"Yes, but I can't prove it. I knew he'd have done anything to prevent her leaving him, to protect his precious reputation of a virile, adventurous writer who lived the books he wrote. It wouldn't do at all to have people know that the great Justin Bradford wasn't man enough to keep his beautiful wife happy. Yes, I think he's very capable of—murder." His mouth looked ugly and tight as it twitched into a travesty of a smile.

"But didn't Bianca's coming to his defense clearly prove he couldn't have—hurt Rosalind?"

"Bianca!" Ennis scoffed, dismissing her with a scornful gesture. "Bianca certainly knew which side her bread was buttered on."

He got up, strode over to the counter where the wine bottle was chilling, picked it up, and brought it over to refill our glasses.

" 'To live a barren sister all your life, Chanting faint hymns to the cold fruitless moon,' " he murmured. "Bianca, my dear Cam, is a very calculating woman despite all her protestations of adoring Rosalind. And Justin owes her his life."

Ennis sat back down, reached to the coffee table, took out a long, filtered cigarette from an ornately carved box, and flicked the rock crystal table lighter to light it.

"Let me give you the picture," he said. "It was a veritable but non-typical ménage à trois at Gull's Glen. Bianca ran the household and took care of the children. Justin wrote his books and Rosalind—most of the time Rosalind did what she wanted. Generally Justin seemed wise enough to allow her a considerable amount of freedom, but then every once in a while he would jerk the string that bound them and pull her back."

Ennis drew deeply on his cigarette before going on.

"It was all his idea to have her portrait painted. As I said, Rosalind was nonchalant about her looks. It was Justin and Bianca who kept at her about them. Justin selected Cole Bernham as the artist he wanted to paint her from an exhibition of Cole's in a San Francisco gallery. Filled with enthusiasm he brought Cole down here. At first he gave him a royal welcome, and seemed pleased at the progress he was making with the portrait. I'm not sure what happened to change his feelings. Cole thought it was

Bianca who sowed the seed of suspicion. She resented how close Cole and Rosalind became, how much they shared, the fun they had together. I think Justin was unaware of it until . . . I mean, he stays closeted writing most of the time he's at Gull's Glen, I mean that's what he comes here for, to write. Anyhow, as Cole told me, one day Justin burst in on them during a sitting and caused a terrible scene. Rosalind was humiliated, and she and Justin had a furious quarrel in front of Cole. There were a lot of old incidents dragged up of other times when Justin's jealousy had been unfounded. She reminded him of them, and in Cole's hearing, told Justin she couldn't live this way any longer. At this point Justin turned on Cole, demanded he get out, that he didn't want him there any longer whether or not the painting was finished."

Ennis leaned forward and crushed out his cigarette in the large conch shell he used as an ashtray.

"Cole came here afterward. He was terribly upset, and in telling me about the scene with Justin, he also confessed he was in love with Rosalind, that he was going to ask her to leave Justin and go away with him. I told him he was a fool. Justin would never let Rosalind go. He had too much ego for one thing. Besides, I think he did love her in his own peculiar, possessive way.

"Well, Cole was stubborn, convinced that Rosalind loved him, too. At this point, I had to leave. I told Cole he could stay here until he had things settled with Justin. He was determined to see Rosalind again; he especially wanted the portrait. It was the best thing he'd ever done, he told me."

Ennis stopped talking abruptly. He sat there, staring into his wineglass.

"And then—" I prompted.

He looked at me almost blankly. "And then—Rosalind was found at the foot of the cliff. Dead."

"How did Cole die?"

"After the inquest, when the jury ruled her death accidental, and Cole was driving back to San Francisco, his car skidded out of control on a blind curve—killed him instantly. The highway patrol said the car was going at an excessive speed. I think it was deliberate. I think it was suicide."

There was a lingering silence, broken at length by Ennis jumping to his feet, and saying, "This is a horrible way to begin an evening that should be pleasurable. My apologies, Cam. This has been in the worst possible taste, dragging out all these old horror stories. I'm going to do my best to turn this evening around, all right? First, we'll have a change of music." He marched over to the stereo, pulled out a drawer of tapes and began examining them.

After that there could not have been a more thoughtful or charming host. Ennis was knowledgeable on all sorts of subjects. We discussed books, music, and theater. He had seen all the plays I wanted to see, attended concerts regularly, and had traveled in Japan and Egypt. He had even lived in Paris for six months. He was, I discovered, a very exciting, interesting man.

I was surprised when I noticed the time.

"Must you go?" he asked. "It's still early."

When I said I did, Ennis said ruefully, "I'd offer to drive you straight to your door, but you know there's no access from my driveway to Gull's Glen, and Justin has his gates locked at midnight. You can't get onto the property without setting off his electronic alarms as well as those hounds of the Baskervilles he keeps as guard dogs. But I'll walk you up those treacherous stairs to your cottage."

I looked around for my jacket. I felt Ennis place it on my shoulders, letting his hands stay there for a moment with slight pressure.

"It's been a marvelous evening, Cam. You are a most accommodating guest. I hope I haven't bored you with all my own travels, thoughts, and talk."

"Oh, no, I found it fascinating. I haven't been many places. I do hope to go to Europe someday," I said a little wistfully, remembering how close I'd come to being there this very summer.

We were standing by the door, our eyes almost level, when he spoke softly, intently. "You're a very interesting person, Cameron. Rather an enigma. There's something so shy and sort of unsure about you which is rather surprising for someone so talented," he said musingly. "I don't believe I've ever met a woman with so little guile. Don't you realize it's dangerous to be so open? You could get hurt . . . badly."

"I have been hurt . . . badly," I replied.

I was caught completely off guard when Ennis grabbed both my wrists playfully and brought me close to him. His face was inches from mine, his eyes so near I could see the pupils. Then he closed them and a moment later I felt the warmth of his lips on mine. I had no time to think or resist, only to feel his hands loosen their grip and his arms go around me, drawing me against him.

He kissed me with an assured expertise that, instead of arousing me, slightly repelled me. As I stiffened in his arms, he let me go with a little laugh.

"You were telling the truth. You have been hurt. You're not ready yet for another man," he said smoothly.

But back in the guest cottage I reminded myself that I had responded with great spontaneity to Jeff's kiss. I felt a thrill of remembered warmth at how I had felt in Jeff's arms, my mouth under his. Ennis was wrong. I *was* ready for another love, but not his kind of casual romantic interlude. It probably assuaged his ego to think I was still nursing a broken heart. He could not understand that I just had no intention of indulging in a fleeting, meaningless affair.

Besides, I wondered if Ennis realized it, but sometimes when he was talking about Rosalind, I had the feeling that he might have been a little in love with her himself.

As I got undressed and ready for bed, I kept thinking

about that aspect. I suppose it would have been easy enough for Ennis to live his friend's infatuation with Rosalind vicariously. It was understandable. The more I heard about Rosalind Bradford, the more curious I became. Rosalind, the myth, the woman, was endlessly fascinating.

CHAPTER 19

The evening of the dinner party I felt out of sorts. Again that morning Dortha had sent down word that she was not coming for her sitting. I was growing more and more frustrated with each passing day. I had become fond of Dortha and was really worried about her, but I was also disturbed about staying on at Gull's Glen with so little progress being made on the portrait. If Dortha was going to continue resisting posing, this commission could drag on all summer. If I was to get on with my own plans, I had better set some sort of deadline for finishing it. I decided to try to talk to Justin and tell him of my decision.

Mentally determining to take some kind of positive action made me feel better. I tried to forget that another day's work had been lost as I got dressed for dinner that evening.

I was just clasping on my earrings and coral necklace, trying its effect on the India print dress I'd decided to wear, when I heard rustling in the bushes under my bedroom window. I stood quite still, straining to listen, my heart quickening noticeably. It was not the first time I'd heard strange noises around the cottage at night, but I had never heard them this early. Usually the mysterious, nondefinable sounds occurred after I was in bed at night. Most of the time I brushed them off as my imagination.

In daytime, when I had explored the vicinity of the three cottages, I had discovered there was no access to this part of the property except from the narrow road from the main house, and the two paths. Since the entire estate was fenced and electronically secured, any trespasser would immediately alert even a sleeping household.

By this time I'd managed to convince myself that the nocturnal noises that I'd heard were made by small woodland creatures. But I had to reluctantly admit that since Ennis had mentioned this cottage was the same one used by the artist who had painted Rosalind, I sometimes had an eerie feeling at night. It was nonsense, of course, but the idea had crossed my mind that the cottage could be haunted.

As I stood motionless now, listening, it seemed that what I heard was different from the scuttling sounds that had awakened me before. There was something stealthy about it, as if someone were sneaking around the outside of the cottage.

I hesitated only a moment, then, gathering all my willpower, I grabbed up my flashlight and quickly went out through the living room. I yanked open the front door, stepped outside, and beamed the flashlight in an arc from side to side. I ran around the side of the house where my bedroom was and focused the light in front of me.

There was dead silence, followed almost immediately by a crashing and scuttling of the low bushes under my window. Next I felt the thump of a whiplike movement against my leg. Seconds later a large dog's head thrust itself into my thigh.

"Bruno!" I gasped. "You scared me to death!"

There was more movement and Olivia jumped out.

"Olivia, what are you doing?" I demanded.

"I'm sorry, Cam. I didn't mean to scare you. I was hiding, actually, from Aunt Bianca."

I looked at her. She was rubbing her bare legs where the rough foliage had scratched them with one hand, while trying to juggle a large, unwieldy book held tight against her slim body.

"Come on inside. We better put something on those scratches. Why were you hiding? I don't understand," I asked as she followed me into the cottage.

I went into my bathroom and brought out some lotion. She put down her burden to take it, and I saw it was one of the scrapbooks from Rosalind's collection.

"Yep, it's one of my mother's scrapbooks," she nodded, seeing that I knew. "I was in there looking at them and I heard Aunt Bianca coming. She keeps it locked, you know, and she's the only one with a key. But Aaron and I found a way to get in, through a small sliding window in the back. Sometimes I go in there, look at the costumes, even try on some of the headdresses. The costumes are still too big for me and anyway, Aunt Bianca would have a fit if she knew.

"She *has* taken me in with her sometimes, although my father would hate it if he knew about it. I look a lot like my mother, you know, and do more and more as I get older. And I think I do want to be an actress like she was. Anyway, Aunt Bianca surprised me by coming down this evening and I managed to get out the back way with the book I was looking at. But now I'm afraid she'll come back and find it missing. So, Cam, can I stay here until it's safe? I mean, once you go up to the house, and the guests come and dinner's started, she won't come back down. Then I'll have time to slip back in and replace the book."

There seemed nothing to do but agree, which I did rather reluctantly. I didn't want to be placed in the position of deceiving Bianca, but what else was there to do, I thought, as I left Olivia drinking a Coke and poring over the picture-crammed scrapbook on my sofa.

When I stepped into the hallway of the big house, I heard voices and laughter coming from the living room and saw that the other guests were already assembled. Justin spotted me standing in the doorway and came over at once to take me around and introduce me. There were two couples, Frank and Mae Ellsworth, and Ted and Nell Sparrow.

"You're the artist whose paintings I just discovered in the Framing Shop Gallery," I exclaimed, recognizing Nell's name. "I love your work," I said to her sincerely.

"How nice of you to say so," Nell Sparrow replied. She was a large woman with naturally blond hair wound into a thick figure-eight roll. Her face was strong, the features blunt, the mouth soft and expressive. Her eyes dominated her face, keen and sparkling with interest whether she was talking or listening.

I would have liked to talk more to her about painting but had no chance because Dortha beckoned me, and took me aside to say, "Forgive me, Cam, I know I'm being a problem. But something happened. —I can't go into it now, but I just couldn't bring myself—"

We were interrupted by Justin coming to her side, putting a protective arm around her shoulders, saying affectionately, "Doesn't my girl look lovely tonight, Cam? Maybe you should paint her in this dress."

I agreed with Justin that the ruffled lavender chiffon dress exactly suited Dortha's delicate beauty, but I also noticed her pallor and that there were shadows under her eyes.

There was no further opportunity to speak to Dortha alone because dinner was soon announced and we all went into the dining room. I was delighted to find myself placed next to Nell Sparrow.

The dinner table was beautifully set for eight. White candles under the large hurricane globes cast a silvery light on the gleaming china and centerpiece of white and purple daisies.

The meal was perfect, equally delightful to the eye and taste—coquilles St. Jacques, fresh asparagus, avocado and grapefruit salad, lime mousse for dessert.

The conversation was as light and sparkling as the wine

Justin lavishly poured. This was a group of comfortably familiar friends all in touch with world events and articulately well informed in the areas of literature, art, and the theater. Justin was at his best, and I was happy to see Dortha participating to some degree in the general discussion.

It was interesting to note that Bianca still sat at the other end of the table, acting as hostess, while Dortha sat to Justin's right. None of them seemed to object to the arrangement, I thought; perhaps it's the one they prefer. I noticed several times during dinner that Justin's hand covered Dortha's and he often gazed at her affectionately. They seemed totally devoted.

And yet, some inner questioner nagged, who was Dortha walking on the beach with in the moonlight when Justin thought her asleep in bed? For I felt sure it *was* Dortha I'd seen. You don't observe someone closely day after day, studying their face and figure, making detailed sketches of both, and not recognize that person, even from a distance. I had watched Dortha too closely not to know the way she moved and walked.

As we gathered for coffee in the living room after dinner, Nell Sparrow sought me out. "I would love to have you come for a visit," she said, "and see some of my other paintings in my home studio, if you can get away from your work here some afternoon."

I was thrilled by her invitation and said I would love to come.

"How about tomorrow, then?" she went on. "I stop working at noon or thereabouts. Any time in the afternoon is fine. We live quite near here. It's secluded from the road, although not quite so much as Gull's Glen. There's a sign at the bottom of the road, you can't miss it. It's called—would you believe—Sparrow's Nest?" She laughed a chiming laugh. "My husband, the staid doctor, gets a little whimsical at times."

"I find it very interesting you're married to a doctor,"

I said. "I was once told your two worlds were poles apart, too separate to coexist." I couldn't help watching her reaction.

"Whoever told you that didn't know what they were talking about," Nell said emphatically. "It's the best of all possible combinations. Since I'm absorbed in my painting, I don't get bored, lonely, or irritated at the hours he keeps, like so many other doctor's wives I know. Neither do I have time to get into the kind of mischief some of them do . . . ." She laughed again. "As a matter of fact, Ted's associates envy him. I am always readying an exhibit or entering a show and can't spend all his money going shopping in the city or dragging him on cruises."

Doug Staley should hear this, I thought with a kind of ironic amusement. Surprisingly, even with the proof that Doug's defense about breaking our engagement did not hold up in reality, it didn't hurt anymore. Somehow the thought of Doug himself had lost its power to distress me. In the next few minutes I found out why. I was called to the phone and the minute I picked up the receiver and heard Jeff Maxwell's voice, my heart responded with a quickened beat.

"I hope I didn't interrupt anything," he said, "but I just wanted to make our date for tomorrow night definite. We're still on, aren't we?"

"Oh, yes, I'm looking forward to it," I answered.

"Wonderful. Shall I come for you about seven?"

"No, I'll drive in and meet you," I replied.

There was a slight pause.

"You're sure? It's no problem for me to come."

"Well, I've been invited to Nell Sparrow's tomorrow afternoon, and I'll just come in from there," I explained.

"Okay, then. Do you want to come to the store afterward?"

"That's fine. I'll see you then, Jeff."

"Cam—" he said.

"Yes?"

"Just that—" He paused. "I'm really looking forward to being with you."

"Me, too," I said, and when I hung up, I was smiling.

When I got back to the living room, the Sparrows were leaving. Dr. Sparrow had an early schedule the next day. I decided to leave too, and Justin insisted on walking back to the cottage with me, saying he needed the exercise and fresh air after all the wine and the heavy meal. Actually I felt he wanted to talk to me privately, and I was right.

"I had a chance to speak to Ted alone for a moment tonight," he said. "He assures me there is nothing he can see wrong with Dortha. Of course, he says unless I could get her into his office for a checkup, he can't be sure. But he says her color is good, and he doesn't see what I'm concerned about." He paused. "But you and I know different, don't we, Cam? Dortha is troubled. I wish I knew why."

At the cottage he opened the door for me, reached in, and snapped the wall light switch that turned on the lamps.

"I guess you still won't let me have a look at the portrait?" he asked rather pleadingly.

"I like to wait until a painting is further along before I let anyone see it," I parried.

He caught sight of the red dress hanging by my easel. I'd picked it up from the floor where Dortha had dropped it the day she was so upset. He went over to it and touched it tenderly, stroking its shimmering folds.

"She is so beautiful," he sighed. "She was like a child with excitement when we bought this in Paris. We were so happy then—" His voice broke a little, then his face settled into firm lines and he said determinedly, "And we will be again, in spite of—" he stopped abruptly, then continued "—in spite of anything."

I couldn't help wondering if he had meant to finish the sentence, *in spite of Bianca.*

After Justin left, I thought about Bianca. I'd watched

her for the past few hours, and it was very clear that she relished her role. She played the part of chatelaine of the manor to perfection. *She enjoys it all,* I thought without too much surprise. She had a taste of power here and was not about to willingly relinquish it. Not to Dortha, not to anyone.

CHAPTER 20

The next morning I got up with a new sense of well-being. I looked out the window and saw that it was a splendid day. The sea sparkled like a giant sapphire with small rippling whitecaps as far as you could see. My conversation with Nell Sparrow had been stimulating and inspiring. It was good to talk to another artist.

I felt more optimistic about the portrait too. Dortha had seemed lovely and relaxed the night before, and I knew she was feeling more comfortable with me. The idea of doing the informal portrait first had been a good idea. It had given Dortha the experience of sitting, and she seemed pleased with the results. The formal one, which we were doing mainly to comply with Justin's insistence on her wearing the red Paris gown, was going well now, too, I thought. I felt confident that things would progress better from now on.

But about a half-hour later, about an hour before Dortha was scheduled to come, I saw Justin coming along the wooded path striding toward the cottage. There was something about him that provoked a twinge of pity and at the same time a pang of apprehension. Was it premonition or was I just becoming used to some new complication every day?

I sighed as I went to open the door. Would this portrait ever be finished? I knew with some inner certainty that Justin had come to tell me Dortha would not be sitting for me.

In a few curt words Justin told me that Dortha had awakened with a headache and felt she could not come to pose this morning. His heavy brows were drawn together over his steel gray eyes, his forehead furrowed, and his mouth grim. I recalled Olivia's comments about her father being furious and Bianca's thinly veiled remarks about Justin's temper.

"I was just about to have a cup of coffee," I told him. "It's freshly brewed. Why don't you join me?"

For some reason I felt instinctively that he needed to talk, to relieve some of the tension I sensed in him. But even as he sat down, his whole body spoke of inner turbulence tightly controlled. He leaned forward, both hands clasped tensely in front of him. I poured coffee and set it on the tray in front of him. Absentmindedly he added sugar and cream, stirring them into his cup silently.

"Do you think—" I began hesitantly "—that we should perhaps postpone the portrait for a while? Dortha seems to hate sitting. I feel she is still resisting the idea, and we may not be able to get the best portrait under the circumstances. Perhaps I could come back later this summer—"

I didn't have a chance to finish. Justin's reaction was so abrupt it startled me. His voice interrupted me, cracking like a whip.

"No! The painting must be finished now. You must stay. Never mind about Dortha. I'll handle her. She'll sit for the portrait if I—no matter what!"

His anger was like summer lightning, vivid, sudden, frightening, gone as quickly as it came. But the memory of it lingered. Was it possible there was another side of Justin, as Ennis had hinted? Was he cruel, ruthless, unforgiving? Capable of violence? Unconsciously I shuddered, remembering Rosalind's death.

I was glad I had made plans for the afternoon and evening. It would be good for me to get completely away from Gull's Glen for a while.

I drove south along the highway, my mind still turning over the scene with Justin, one thought tumbling on another, over and over. I had seen a side of Justin that morning that I had not seen before. It had only been a glimpse, but enough to wonder if what Ennis said and Bianca hinted at were true of him.

On the other hand, I countered, Justin was a writer. He had a mercurial temperament often found in creative people. His enthusiasm could quickly turn into brusqueness and depression. I'd seen it in artists. Then, too, for reasons of her own, possibly her blind devotion to her dead sister, Bianca might be trying to give me an unfavorable image of Justin.

To me Justin had been consistently courteous and pleasant, if lately more detached, preoccupied, and troubled. He adored Dortha and had an obsession about having her portrait painted, that was all. He was also worried about her health, her state of mind; with all that had happened recently, it was perfectly natural that he should be on edge.

Just then I noticed a small, distinctive sign, SPARROW'S NEST, and braked, grateful for Nell's invitation. She had said not to bother to call, that she stopped working in the early afternoon. That was what I needed, a visit with someone like Nell Sparrow to get my mind off the troubles at Gull's Glen.

I shifted into low gear and started up the twisting road. Why did everyone in this area make their homes so inaccessible, I wondered, knowing the answer even as I asked it. I saw the roof of the house over the tops of gnarled cypress trees twisting from the rocks along the drive leading to it. A weathered redwood gate stood slightly ajar, and as I got out of the car and pushed it open, I saw that it led into a garden.

There was a small bronze statue of Pan playing his pipes, turned green by the sea air, under the shelter of a bonsai. A Japanese stone lantern was reflected in the small pond in the center.

The house had the pure, simple lines of Oriental architecture, and as I waited in the tiny courtyard after ringing the bell beside the paneled front door, I was conscious of the serenity of this setting broken only by the wind stirring the cypress and, far away, the faint roar of the ocean.

A few minutes later the door was opened by Nell, whose spontaneous delight at seeing me dismissed any doubt I might have had about my decision to come.

Inside, the house was less austere than the garden. It was filled with warm touches that reflected Nell's personality. It had color, warmth, and paintings by local artists. She took me out to her studio, which had a wonderful view of the ocean with coastal mountains in the background. Afterward we settled down for tea at a table setting that looked like one of her own paintings with a Japanese teapot with a spray of apple blossoms in its design, a bowl of ruby-red strawberries to dip in sugar, a plate of tiny sesame seed cookies, and a small dish of cloved lemon slices.

It seemed only natural that the subject of Dortha's portrait came up almost at once. Nell Sparrow seemed someone to trust and gradually I began to tell her some of my difficulties, mainly about Dortha's reluctance to sit for me.

"I met her for the first time the other evening," Nell said slowly. "Of course I've known Justin and knew Rosalind for years. She is a lovely creature, but I sensed an inner uncertainty, a tension. But perhaps that's only to be expected, under the circumstances." A long pause followed.

"I'd hate to be anyone who would try to replace Rosalind in that household. Justin worshiped her, the children adored her, her sister—well, Bianca was the only mother

Rosalind ever had, and of course, you can imagine that relationship. . . ."

Nell refilled my cup and offered me more lemon. Her smooth brow knotted in a worried frown as she continued. "I just hope—for his own sake—Justin doesn't make the same mistake with Dortha that he made with Rosalind. He made her life unbearable with his jealousy.

"Rosalind had a restless, outgoing nature. She had to be doing all the time. She loved people. There were basic differences in their personalities that an observer would have known spelled doom to their marriage from the outset. However, they were deeply in love . . . at least at first. Justin's possessive, excessive love began to strangle Rosalind. He tried to curtail her activities, her friendships, her freedom. I saw what it was doing to their relationship, I think, even before Rosalind began to tug at his hold on her.

"Our Shakespeare group seemed to be the catalyst for the buildup at the end. Yet it started out as such fun." Nell shook her head sadly. "You know Rosalind was principally a Shakespearean actress, except for a brief stint in Hollywood? Oh, yes, she trained in Ashland for years at the Shakespeare Theater, and Bianca had aimed her ambitions toward England and then, of course, to Broadway. But she met Justin. . . .

"Bianca never let anyone forget—especially Justin—that Rosalind gave up her career to marry him. Of course Justin has been enormously successful but even so, Bianca, well, back to the Shakespeare Seven. That's how it began, seven of us, all Shakespeare buffs. We met regularly, usually once a week at each other's homes. We'd read aloud from the plays, and we began to talk about a week-long Shakespeare festival to be held here every year, like the Bach Festival. It was Rosalind's idea, and as she always did, she became wildly enthusiastic about putting it on."

"Yes, I heard about that," I said, "but not about the

group you mention, the Shakespeare Seven." I remembered what Jeff had told me.

"Well, that of course was the core of it, our intimate group. We were all very close friends, enjoyed getting together, and of course sharing our interest.

"Most often we played what we called the Shakespeare game. One person would give a quote, the others would try to place it, by speaker, by play, or if it was from a sonnet, quote the ending verse. Justin hated it when the game spilled over to social gatherings, as it sometimes did. He felt totally left out by this sort of thing.

"Justin was bored by the whole thing; but more significant, I think, jealous of Rosalind's involvement in it and with us. You know, Justin is a self-educated man. He made it plain that he thought the group was a kind of elite, phony, culture-happy group of pseudo-intellectuals. You've read Justin's books?"

I shook my head, feeling a little guilty that I hadn't.

"No great loss, unless you enjoy lots of macho adventure, a sprinkling of sex, and pages of derring-do action. He's strictly a commercial writer. He figured out what sells, found a formula, and has stuck to it for years. Nothing changes but names and setting. That's why he resented Rosalind getting so deeply interested and involved in a community effort like the proposed Shakespeare Festival. He wanted her strictly for himself. He didn't want anything to interfere with his life-style, which was to travel most of the year finding exotic settings for his books, then to come here from May until October to write, then be off again.

"The truth is, he wanted Rosalind's attention exclusively. He wanted her to be at his beck and call, ready to come and go when he wanted, and he resented her having any interest he wasn't part of. Of course, we all knew this, and we had a kind of inside joke about it. Privately we said Justin was playing Othello to Rosalind's Desdemona, never realizing how tragically true that analogy was to become." Nell's voice wavered, and she put down her teacup with a sigh.

Even after I left Nell's, all she had told me lingered in my mind.

Rosalind! It seemed that wherever I turned, there she was. A multifaceted image of her had begun to emerge. But what was fact, what was fantasy?

As I turned my car toward Carmel, I was glad I would be with Jeff that evening. I was glad to put behind me, if just for a few hours, the mysterious aura that surrounded Gull's Glen like the fabled fog.

CHAPTER 21

Jeff was waiting for me when I pulled up in front of his store. He seemed ridiculously happy to see me, as though it had been ages instead of only two days since we had been together.

"I thought I'd cash in on the raincheck you promised and take you down to Cannery Row. I thought we'd have dinner at the Steinbeck Lobster Grotto, if that's okay with you? I haven't been there myself since it's fairly new, but some friends told me it was great."

"That sounds fine," I agreed.

"Did you have a pleasant afternoon?" he asked me once we had changed cars and he headed his TR-6 south on the highway out of Carmel.

"Very. Nell is so talented besides being a charming, interesting person."

"I suppose you talked shop all afternoon," Jeff said in a teasing tone.

"Not entirely. As a matter of fact, we talked a lot about Rosalind Bradford."

"That's right, I'd forgotten they were good friends," Jeff commented. "Well, did you learn anything new?"

"Maybe. Just enough to make me thoroughly confused." I frowned. "Everyone gives me a different picture of Rosalind, but they all seem to have the same idea about Justin being overly possessive, jealous, that sort of thing."

Jeff shrugged. "I wouldn't know."

"Ennis Shelby, for instance, seems particularly hostile toward Justin," I continued.

Jeff gave me a quick glance. "Oh, by the way, how was your dinner with him?" he asked. "Did he show you his photographs or was he too busy making a pass?"

"Jeff!" I remonstrated.

He laughed. "Scratch that. It's none of my business anyhow. How's the portrait coming, to change the subject."

"That's something I'd rather not discuss. At least not right now," I answered quietly.

"Sure," Jeff agreed immediately, switching our conversation to a variety of subjects, impressing me more and more that he was a person of wide interests and keen intelligence. The more I was with him, the more I was attracted and the more comfortable I felt.

When we arrived at Cannery Row, it was far from how I had pictured it from Steinbeck's novels. It had been prettied up for the tourists, as Jeff had warned.

The interior of the restaurant where Jeff had made our reservation was most attractive. It had been cleverly divided into separate dining spaces by ship's rigging and various platforms which afforded a view from every table. When we were seated and I looked out the window, I was delighted to see some sea otters playing on the rocks and in the water of the small cove just below.

The waiter who brought our menus reminded us that fresh fish was the specialty of the house, so we decided to try abalone served with artichokes stuffed with herbed rice. Jeff ordered a Chenin Blanc, and while we waited for our dinners, we sipped its cool, crisp flavor as we watched the playful otters.

When our salads and a basket of warm crusty French bread was placed before us, I realized how hungry I was.

"Didn't you work at all today?" Jeff asked after a while. "Is something wrong up at Gull's Glen, Cam, something about the portrait? I have a feeling—" He stopped, looking at me intently. "You're not giving up, are you? Don't tell me you're leaving before it's finished?"

When I didn't answer right away, he persisted. "Come on, Cam, I know there's something, please tell me."

"Well—" I hesitated.

"I know there must be something. It's not like you to do something impulsive, not when you're committed to a project."

Reminding myself to ask him sometime how he felt he knew me well enough to make that kind of judgment, I decided to confide in Jeff. Instinctively I knew I could trust him.

Gradually all the strange, unexplained incidents of my stay at Gull's Glen came out. He listened attentively. The only time he showed any real reaction was when I mentioned Ennis.

"In a way I wish I didn't know about what happened to the artist who was painting Rosalind. Ennis told me all about it. He didn't mean to upset me. I'm sure he thought it might help me to know what happened. He's been a friend of the Bradfords for years and seems genuinely concerned."

Jeff raised his eyebrows.

"You don't agree?" I asked.

"It's not that I don't agree that he's known the Bradfords for years," Jeff began. "It's just that I don't think there's any love lost between him and Justin. Cole Burnham was his friend, you know."

"Yes, I know, but still—" I paused. I felt that Jeff was holding something back, trying to decide whether or not to share it with me. "What is it, Jeff?"

A thoughtful expression came over his face. "It's that I always had the feeling Ennis was in love with Rosalind himself," he said slowly, then shrugged. "But then, from what I hear, almost every man around here was in love with her at one time or another."

"You?" I asked, half-teasingly.

Jeff smiled and shook his head. "Nope. Not me." He looked at me for a long moment, his eyes leveling in a steady gaze. "*Me*—I'm in love with *you.*"

He reached across the table for my hand, and I did not draw it away.

"How could you possibly be in love with me?" I asked, incredulous. "We've only known each other a few weeks."

"Is there some sort of set timetable for falling in love?"

He kept smiling, that slow smile of his, the one that started in his eyes, and put out his hand to touch my cheek. Softly, he said, "You need me to lighten up your life a little, Cam. You're much too serious."

A light misty rain was falling when we came out of the restaurant, and by the time we drove back to Carmel it was getting foggy.

"I wish you'd let me drive you home," Jeff said, scowling, as I got my car keys out of my purse. "I can bring your VW out to you tomorrow, no trouble."

"I'll be fine, Jeff, don't worry. I'm used to driving in the fog. I've lived in the San Francisco area for three years, you know."

"You're so darn independent," he said softly, pulling me into his arms. He kissed me with a sweet intensity that deepened and lengthened as I responded. "I've been wanting to do that all night," he whispered and kissed me again. This time we both lost track of time. I could feel his heart pounding against mine as I returned kiss for kiss.

"I've got to go." I said at last.

"Don't go. Stay with me tonight."

I shook my head. "No, Jeff. It's—well, too soon."

"I do love you. Don't you believe that?" he asked gently.

"I don't know, I mean, yes, I believe you do, and yet I guess I can't quite believe any of this is real."

"Believe me, what I'm feeling is very real." His arms tightened around me. We kissed again, a long, lingering kiss.

Finally he let me go. I felt a little disoriented, dazed by my own feelings.

A few minutes later I was on the highway headed for Gull's Glen without really knowing how I'd got there. It was foggier than I'd realized. Ghostly wisps, eerily floating and evaporating like so many wraiths in front of my headlights, made it necessary for me to go slowly.

I glanced at my wristwatch in the light from the dashboard. At midnight the electronically controlled gates to Gull's Glen property automatically went on the security alarm system. I had left a message that I would be gone for the evening, but still I didn't want to wake everyone by coming in after they were locked.

I peered anxiously through the mist, not wanting to miss the turnoff to Gull's Glen. I turned on my windshield wipers, as the rain and fog were clouding my vision. Finally, with some relief, I glimpsed the sign.

Making the turn, I started up the steep, winding road past the silent, dark main house onto the narrower one that led back to the three guest cottages in the wood.

I braked the car in front of my cottage, and sat there for a few minutes just thinking about the evening and what had happened between Jeff and me. Could he really be in love with me? Could what I was feeling mean that I had fallen in love with him? Could it have happened this soon after Doug, I wondered, even when I had promised myself it would be a long time before I let myself get involved in a relationship again?

Only time would tell. But then I wouldn't be in Carmel much longer—just until Dortha's portrait was finished. Whenever that would be, I sighed, remembering all the problems.

I got out of the car, searched for my door key, and unlocked the cottage door.

But the minute I stepped inside, I knew something was wrong. I stood quite still, listening for I knew not what. Every muscle, every nerve strained. Outside, the rain beat a gentle tattoo and then came the sound of a window banging a dull drumbeat.

I felt an eerie apprehensive chill. I walked cautiously into the middle of the room and slowly pivoted, looking around me.

Then I saw it.

The red dress, like some horrible effigy swinging from the hanger on which I'd placed it, danced a frenzied ballet in the gusts of misty wind blowing in from the open window.

It was ruined, sodden, stained, and streaked. Its once shimmering folds hung in violated elegance.

Shocked, I took it over to the light and examined it. It was destroyed beyond repair, I thought, heartsick.

What could I do?

After the first shock, a grim realization dawned on me. Suddenly I remembered I had not left the dress where I had just found it. I was sure I had replaced it in its plastic cover and hung it near my easel on the other side of the room. I put the dress down and went back over to the window. Here I made a horrifying discovery.

I gasped. Dortha was right. Someone was out to hurt her, to frighten her, to destroy her and Justin's marriage. Even, perhaps, to destroy her.

CHAPTER 22

That night I tossed and turned endlessly. I kept asking myself who could have done such a dreadful thing. The small piece of wood, so cleverly whittled and propped so that the window would stay open and the wind and rain blow in on the dress, was evidence that it had been a deliberate act.

Relentlessly I went down the line of possibilities. It came down to Aaron, that strange, hostile boy. He made no secret of his antipathy to Dortha, his rebellion toward his father. How more could he hurt Justin than by destroying something that belonged to his new stepmother?

The last time I looked at my travel clock on the bedside table, it was nearly three. I don't remember when I finally fell into an exhausted sleep.

In the morning a gray sheet of fog enveloped the cottage and shrouded the view of the ocean. For a few moments I lay in bed, not wanting to believe it had really happened. Maybe it had been some kind of awful nightmare.

I got up warily, pulled on my robe, shoved my feet into slippers, and went out into the living room. With a jolt of horror I saw the dress again and knew it had not been a bad dream. The question was, what should I do now?

I brewed coffee, all the time glaring at the crumpled satin, stained and darkened, ruined beyond repair. Or was it?

Just then an idea flashed to mind. The day Bianca had showed me Rosalind's costumes I had remarked on their beautiful condition. She had explained that although stage costumes are usually made of durable materials, they take much wear and tear in the long run of a play. She told me she sent Rosalind's costumes to a firm in San Francisco specializing in cleaning and restoring delicate fabrics; they used a unique preserving process. Bianca had recalled an instance when something had been spilled down the front of a white satin Juliet costume. They had driven to San Francisco with it and within hours it had been restored to its pristine beauty, in time for the next performance.

Of course I had not thought to ask Bianca the name of the company. There had been no need then. Now with this emergency I wished desperately that I had.

I was torn. I certainly did not want to tell Bianca about the vandalized dress or alarm Justin and Dortha unless I was forced to do so.

How could I find out the name of the San Francisco firm who did such miracles, get the dress to them and back before anyone else knew about this act of diabolic vandalism?

Then it struck me that the local dramatic group in Carmel, the actors or managers, surely would know the name of an establishment who did theatrical costume cleaning and repair.

I put down my coffee cup and got up. At least that was a possibility.

This time I would have to be the one to postpone Dortha's sitting. But how could I manage it?

It was still early. No one in the main house would be up yet. I could leave a note that a personal emergency required me to be away for the day. It wasn't the kind of thing I liked doing, having been brought up to believe that to withhold the truth is the same as lying. But this time I felt justified.

I wrapped the still-damp dress carefully in tissue paper I found in one of the bureau drawers, and slipped it into a cardboard suit box I found on one of the closet shelves. I carried it out to my car and placed it on the backseat. I then taped my note to the front door of the cottage and drove as quietly as possible past the big house, down the narrow road to the highway, and then on to Carmel.

As I went through town I suddenly realized it was far too early for anything to be open. I'd have to wait until someone came into the Studio-Theater, which might be noon, knowing the hours most actors keep. I drove around looking for someplace I could wait. I spotted an attractive little restaurant serving Danish pastry and coffee. I had no problem finding a parking place at this hour. I got out, locked the car, and went into the shop fragrant with the smells of freshly ground coffee and baked delicacies. To my surprise, Ennis Shelby was seated at one of the tables.

Simultaneously we asked each other, "What are you doing here?" Then we both laughed. He rose and waved me over to his table.

I slipped into the seat opposite him and, before I could order, a smiling waiter brought me a steaming mug of dark, rich coffee.

"I'm on my way to San Francisco," Ennis said. "But what got you up and out on this dreary, foggy morning?"

Within minutes I'd told him the whole awful story.

"I really don't know what to do," I said. "I don't want to cause Dortha any more distress. I'm beginning to believe it's the kind of malicious mischief a vindictive teenager like Aaron might use to get even with his father. I don't want to cause trouble for anyone, I simply want to finish my portrait and frankly . . . get out." I sighed. "That's why I'm in town. I want to get the name of the firm Bianca told me about that does repairs for theatrical costumes. I hoped to get it from someone at the Studio-Theater, but of course they're not open this early—and of course, I have to get it done before anyone finds out."

"You can't tell what time the people at the theater will be in," Ennis said thoughtfully. "I have a suggestion. I could take it with me when I drive to the city this morning. It would be a matter of looking through the yellow pages in the phone directory, and making a few inquiries.

I can probably walk it over or have them pick it up at my studio. If they do give twenty-four-hour service, I can bring it back with me the day after tomorrow, and no one will be the wiser. That is, if you still intend not telling anyone."

"Oh, Ennis, could you? That way it can be done without my having to explain things to people who wouldn't understand that I don't want this to be a source of gossip about the Bradfords," I explained gratefully.

Ennis put a finger up to his lips and said solemnly, " 'The better part of valour is discretion'—of which I'll be the soul!"

"You're a lifesaver," I said. My relief took the form of instant hunger, and I ordered pancakes with loganberry syrup.

As we transferred the box containing the dress from my VW to Ennis's sleek, black Ferrari, I remarked, "At least it's going in style." Then, "Ennis, how can I ever thank you?"

"I'll think of some way." He smiled and something curious flickered in his eyes as they seemed to study me.

"I hope it won't be too expensive," I said.

He raised his eyebrows. "Do you mean the dress or your repayment?"

"Neither one." I laughed a little nervously. "Should I give you a check now?"

"Let's wait and see what it will cost." He smiled wickedly and added, "The dress, I mean. I'll have to think about your repayment."

"I hope that will be negotiable," I countered, attempting lightness.

"We'll see. But don't worry. I'm sure everything will work out satisfactorily."

I stood on the curb and watched him drive off, taking my most immediate problem with him. What luck it had been to run into Ennis like that, and on his way to the city too.

As the Ferrari turned the corner and disappeared out of sight, I took a long breath, and unconsciously crossed my fingers. Hopefully by this time tomorrow, as Ennis had said, everything would work out satisfactorily.

I had the whole day to myself, I remembered, because of the note I'd left. Besides, I didn't want to answer any questions until the dress had been returned safely. I'd have to remain away from Gull's Glen all day.

Jeff was just opening up when I sauntered into the sunlit court where his shop was located. I had to laugh at his expression when I said, "Good morning."

"What are you doing here?" he asked in astonishment.

"That's the second time today I've been asked that question," I answered with a smile. "I'm playing hooky, that's what."

"Well, let's play hooky together." He grinned. With that he immediately turned over the open sign he had just put on the door, and motioned me inside.

"I will now show you my secret entrance and then we can make our plans for the day," he said mysteriously. Giving me a wink as he took hold of my hand, he led me behind the counter and through a door.

I found myself in a narrow hallway with a circular iron staircase.

"Come on, I'll show you where I live."

I followed Jeff up the stairs to a loftlike apartment with beamed ceilings and stained-wood window frames, from which we could look out on the panorama of Carmel village. I looked around me with interest. Jeff's living quarters were very much like him, a combination of warmth, individuality, and a surprisingly sophisticated taste in paintings, furnishings, and books.

He poured coffee into pottery mugs, and handing me one, asked, "Tell me, Cam, what was your childhood fantasy of playing hooky?"

I thought for a minute. "I don't know. A party, maybe, or the circus or a picnic."

"I can't provide the circus, regretfully, but the picnic I can manage. We can make it a party. And I know the perfect place to go."

He put down his mug, reached up on one of the open shelves, and brought down a slant-topped wicker basket.

"See, I'm ready for every contingency." He grinned.

"I can't believe you've got the fixings for a picnic on hand," I said.

"Not exactly, but I know where to get them. Let me just put a couple of glasses, some napkins, and some cutlery in here." As he talked, he began packing items in the basket. "Salt, pepper, mustard, a cutting board, butter—there, that will do it. We'll pick up the rest of the things on the way," he said. He grabbed up a woven blanket from one of the deep couches that flanked the stone fireplace, and asked, "Have you got a warm sweater with you or should I bring along an extra one? We're going to stay to see the sunset and it may be breezy down at the beach."

Within another few minutes we were in his car easing along streets that were just beginning to show morning activity. We stopped at a wonderful little market where the proprietors knew Jeff. He carried on a joking conversation with them as he expertly selected two kinds of cheese, a loaf of French bread, a bottle of wine, and some luscious-looking peaches and grapes.

"Now, we're all set," he said. "And while I get us to this really special place where we're going to spend the day, why not tell me the real reason you're running away from Gull's Glen?"

Briefly I told him the dreadful story, and about the coincidental meeting with Ennis Shelby that morning.

"Good old Ennis to the rescue, eh?" Jeff said sardonically.

I looked over at him quizzically, surprised at his tone of voice.

"Why, Jeff, you sound—well, I don't know how."

"Jealous?" he supplied, frowning.

"Well, I don't know that that's the word I'd use—"

"Well, it's what I am," he said grimly. He reached over and took my hand, squeezing it hard.

"Foolish as that may sound, I guess I wish I'd been the one to help you. You see, Cameron Forrest, I meant what I said the other night. I'm in love with you. I want to always be the one you turn to in any kind of emergency. Or for that matter for anything, anywhere, any time."

"Oh, Jeff," I said softly.

He gave my hand another long squeeze, then said cheerfully, "And now I suggest we leave all your troubles at Gull's Glen behind and enjoy ourselves completely, just the two of us."

It took us a little less than an hour to drive to where Jeff's secret beach was. We parked off the road, then walked to a path that was almost hidden by stunted pine trees. We scrambled down it. At times it was so steep I had to hold on to the thick bushes that grew on either side to slow myself and keep myself from toppling on top of Jeff, who was leading the way. The slender crescent of this secret beach was protected by great jagged rocks and there was a small running stream in which Jeff placed our wine to cool. He spread the blanket, and we sat down.

"I wish I'd brought my sketch book," I sighed. I looked out at the sparkling dark-blue water. "And a swim suit," I added.

"There's always skinny dipping," he teased.

"Jeff!"

"I was kidding. It's too dangerous here to swim, anyway. There's a very dangerous undertow." He leaned over and kissed me, then smiled. "That's one of the reasons I love you. There are very few girls nowadays who still blush. You're adorable, Cam."

"I'm hungry, that's what I am," I said, a little flustered.

"That's easily remedied," Jeff said, opening the basket.

We ate heartily of the French bread and cheese and sipped on the nicely chilled wine.

"I feel like a decadent Roman reclining here, eating and drinking on my own private beach," I said, holding up a bunch of grapes and biting one off with my teeth. "Don't you feel like Caesar?"

"Caesar should be so lucky," he said slowly. "Cam, don't go back to the city after you finish Dortha's portrait. Stay here and marry me."

I turned to look at him. He was regarding me with steady, serious eyes.

"I love you. I know you'd be happy in Carmel. I'd make you happy." He paused. "Do you think—could you possibly feel about me the same way I do about you?"

"Jeff, I have plans. They don't include marriage. Not for a long time—maybe never. I wouldn't want you to think—"

His hand caressed the back of my neck. I felt a tingle at his touch that made my heart speed up. Gently he moved my head to look at him, then he bent and kissed me. His lips were warm, and tasted of salt and wine. His arms went around me and gathered me into the curve of his body.

"Never mind answering me now, Cam. I'll wait until you're ready. I didn't mean to get so serious today. Today is to enjoy." Jeff brushed my hair from my face, and kissed me again, this time lightly. I settled my head on his shoulder, and drowzy from the sun and the wine, I felt my eyes close. Gradually, with the sound of the surf in my ears and the cry of distant seagulls, I fell asleep in Jeff's embrace.

I don't know how much later I stirred. I was lying on the blanket alone, with Jeff's sweater over me. I sat up, and as the sweater slipped from my shoulders, I shivered. The wind from the ocean had come up, and I knew from the shadows of the rocks above that it was getting late. Down by the shore I saw Jeff's tall figure silhouetted against the brilliant pre-sunset sky. I felt a lifting sensation as I looked at him. Instinctively I knew I was falling in love with him.

As if he had sensed my thoughts, he turned, waved,

then came running back up the sand to me. His arm around me holding me close to him, together we watched the sun slide down the sky and sink into the sea in a blaze of glory. Reluctantly we gathered up our picnic basket, folded the blanket, and climbed back up the hill to the car.

It was dark when we arrived in Carmel. Hand in hand, we climbed the twisting staircase to Jeff's apartment.

"Hungry?" he asked.

He lit lamps and started a fire in the fireplace.

"Want to look around at the rest of the place while I see what we can have for dinner?" Jeff asked.

Besides the large living room, kitchen and dining area, there were two bedrooms and a bath. The big bedroom was obviously Jeff's, very neat and masculine in colors of rich brown and beige with touches of orange. There was a huge skylight directly over the king-size bed. As I stood in the doorway looking in, I felt Jeff's arms go around my waist. His head bent to rub my cheek gently and he whispered in my ear, "In that bed you can look straight up at the stars. On a really starry night you can see about five hundred thousand. If you don't believe me, you might want to see for yourself."

"Oh, Jeff, you're impossible." I laughed.

He hugged me and laughed, too. Releasing me, he said, "Come out to the kitchen and keep me company while I fry us a couple of hamburgers. Not gourmet, but it's all I can come up with tonight. Unless you'd like to go out somewhere?"

"No, this is fine. Perfect, in fact. Have you got fixings for a salad? I can tear lettuce beautifully," I offered.

We ate on the coffee table in front of the fireplace. Both of us were hungrier than we had realized after the day in the sun and sea air. We did not talk much, didn't seem to need to. It was just warm and comfortable being together.

Jeff insisted on following me back to Gull's Glen in his car.

As we passed the big house, I was surprised to see lights

on in almost every window. It was past eleven, and Justin had made a point of telling me he kept early hours when he was working.

I didn't have much time to think any more about it, as the next half hour was spent saying good night to Jeff. Finally, after another lingering kiss on the doorstep of the cottage, we parted. I let myself in, listened to the sound of his motor as he drove off, then prepared dreamily for bed.

The day with Jeff had been wonderful. I marveled at our easy companionship, how good it felt being with him. I thought of his considerateness, how he thought of anything and everything I would enjoy. I thought of his dark, good looks, his strong features, that slow, sweet smile, the way his eyes had searched my face for a response when he'd told me he loved me, his quiet sense of humor. All in all, he was a very special man, I thought, as I snuggled into the blankets, and drifted off to sleep.

I don't know how long I'd been asleep when something awakened me.

I sat up in bed, instantly alert. Then I saw what it was. A fan-shaped beam of light moved swiftly across my window and back. It came and went twice more. It was as if someone were searching for something. I waited tensely for it to come again. When it didn't, I snatched up my robe and crept to the window, bending low so that if it came again, the arc of light would not catch me in its beam.

I drew back the curtain cautiously so that I could see out without being seen. I squinted out, trying to penetrate the darkness. Then the light shone again, darting quickly back and forth. This time it was two cottages away. Someone was at Rosalind's cottage with a flashlight moving around inside!

Was it Bianca, coming for some ritual vigil? I quickly rejected that idea. Why would she come in the middle of the night like a burglar? She was the only one who had a key, Olivia had told me. But there was that back window that both she and Aaron knew about. Had Olivia come to return the scrapbook without her aunt knowing? It must be one of the youngsters, I decided. Only they would be reckless enough to chance Bianca's wrath.

I started to turn back to bed when something else caught my attention. The light again, this time briefly illuminating the person who held it, as though in juggling something else, whoever it was had beamed it on himself. But all I saw in the brief flash was the outline of a hooded figure. Then the light went out suddenly, and I saw nothing more.

After that it was hard to go back to sleep. All sorts of possibilities popped in and out of my head. Who had it been? It could have been anyone. The hooded Irish cape that hung in the hall was accessible to anyone—man, woman, child. It completely hid the wearer's identity. I had seen everyone at Gull's Glen wear it at one time or another, myself included. I couldn't remember the last time I'd worn it back to this cottage from dinner, or if Dortha, Olivia, Bianca, Justin or even Rachel had returned it for me.

It would be impossible to say who was moving so silently and suspiciously through the night woods on who knew what surreptitious errand.

CHAPTER 23

When I woke the next morning, I had almost forgotten the frightening incident. When I remembered, it was so vague in my mind I wondered if I might have dreamed it. My most pressing thought was the ruined dress. Had Ennis been able to have it repaired? My next thought was that

I would have to go up to the house with an excuse for my absence yesterday.

I got up and looked out of the window. Fog hung like gray sheets from the trees surrounding the cottage, and I had the eerie feeling of being totally cut off.

I tried to shake the feeling as I dressed, fixed myself coffee, and planned what I would say to the Bradfords.

Later, walking along the wooded path to the house, the fog was so thick it shredded as I went forward like a ghostly curtain parting. It reminded me of the mysterious visitor to Rosalind's cottage the night before and I shivered. How strangely real the dead woman seemed.

As I neared the house, I gathered my thoughts into an acceptable explanation for being gone. As it turned out, no excuse was necessary.

When I reached the front driveway, I noticed there was another car parked beside Dortha's cream Jaguar and Justin's vintage Austin-Healy. On the license plate of the unfamiliar sedan, I saw the caduceus, the medical symbol most doctors attach to their vehicles. Was someone ill, I wondered.

Just as I started up the terrace steps, Olivia came running out to meet me. "Oh, Cam," she cried, "Dortha's had an accident. There was an awful row at dinner last night, Aaron and Father! It was terrible and Dortha got very upset. She jumped up from the table and ran out. She was gone a long time and then Father got worried. Everyone went out looking for her. Aaron, too. He took the dogs. He was the one who found her. She'd fallen on the rocks on the seawall path and was unconscious. Father carried her back to the house and called Dr. Sparrow. It was all very dramatic! Actually she wasn't hurt badly, at least not seriously. A sprained ankle, that's all," Olivia concluded with a big sigh.

I hurried into the house to find Bianca talking to Dr. Sparrow and a distraught-looking Justin coming down the stairway. They all assured me that Dortha was not badly hurt. Aside from the sprained ankle, she was bruised and shaken. She had been given a sedative and would probably sleep most of the day.

As I walked back to the guest cottage, I felt that since Dortha's injuries were not critical, the atmosphere of tension that had been palpable was due more to the eerie resemblance of Dortha's accident to Rosalind's fatal fall. There were sinister implications hanging over the incident. I was sure all three—Bianca, Justin, and Ted Sparrow—were acutely aware of them.

Back at my cottage I reheated the coffee and faced the long day stretching drearily ahead of me. I could not work on the portrait and it was too miserable outside to go down to the beach. Even Olivia, whose company I might have sought for lack of anyone else, had plans. She told me when I was up at the house that one of her school friends was visiting her grandmother in Pacific Grove, and Bianca was driving her there to spend the day and stay overnight.

The only positive secondary effects of Dortha's being laid up for a few days was the fact that I would not have to tell anyone about the dress yet. If Ennis had been successful in San Francisco getting it repaired, no one would have to be the wiser.

Still, the question remained: Who had done that terrible thing? All the adults had remarked on Aaron's bravery and resourcefulness the night before as he had hunted for Dortha on the treacherous rocks in the dark. It seemed oddly ironic that he might have sabotaged the portrait for spite, and then risked his own safety to search for her.

I felt lonely and restless. For the first time since I'd arrived at Gull's Glen, I couldn't settle down.

Maybe I'd drive in to Carmel, visit a few art galleries, then stop by and see Jeff. I grabbed my jacket and purse and went out to my car. As I started to unlock it and get in, my foot kicked something. I looked down and saw that it was a small, slim book.

I picked it up to examine its soft gray leather cover, now

limp from being on the soggy ground. It was embossed with a border of gold leaves and the gold letters read *Selections from the Plays and Sonnets of William Shakespeare.* Curious, I opened it and saw this inscription on the fly-leaf:

> No sooner met but they looked; no sooner looked but they loved; no sooner loved but they sighed; no sooner sighed but they asked one another the reason; no sooner knew the reason but they sought the remedy.

Beneath these lines in quotes was scribbled *As You Like It* with a question mark afterward.

Thoughtfully I carried it into the cottage. Whose was it? What was the meaning of the dedication? More to the point, who had dropped it so close to my cottage?

Inside I turned the pages more slowly and carefully. There were several places where words and phrases had been underlined. It was a book that had been exchanged with some significance to both the giver and the recipient; it had been well read. How had it been lost?

Although beautifully bound and expensively printed, the book was the size of a paperback, and could easily be carried in a pocket—and just as easily slip out. Falling on the piny floor of the woods without a sound, it would not be immediately missed.

It had definitely been a gift, the kind one would give to a lover, I thought, as I examined it again. But by whom to whom, and why was it dropped near my cottage?

I curled up on the sofa and began to read through it.

Since I had never studied Shakespeare, I only recognized the most familiar quotations attributed to him. But as I turned the pages of the sonnet section, I found myself stopping to read and savor the hauntingly beautiful verses. The thought struck me that perhaps they were meant to be read only by lovers, shared by people who lived in a world comprised of two.

Then I remembered Nell Sparrow telling me about the *Shakespeare Seven.* Anyone involved in it would be well versed in Shakespeare's works. Besides herself and Rosalind, I realized, she had not mentioned who else was a member of the group. Justin wasn't. Had Bianca been? Who were the five other charter members? It didn't seem likely that the pragmatic Dr. Ted Sparrow would be. Who then? Had this book belonged to Rosalind? Whoever the mysterious midnight prowler at her cottage had been, might he have dropped it?

I put the book face down on the coffee table and got up impatiently. There had been so many unexplained mysteries since I'd come to Gull's Glen, like so many pieces in a puzzle, scattered tantalizingly in every direction. Would they ever all fit into a pattern?

All I had wanted to do when I'd arrived was to paint a portrait of Dortha Bradford. Now I was entangled in all sorts of complicated relationships.

And then there was Jeff.

I thought of our kisses of the night before, how I had responded to his lovemaking with spontaneous gladness. I had felt the wonderful joy of loving and being loved, of knowing with an inner certainty that this was what I'd been waiting for all my life. But at the same time I had denied that love.

I walked back and forth across the room, then stood at the window where the heavy fog now blocked out the sight of the sea.

I put the kettle on to boil for tea, went over to my easel, looked at Dortha's painting for some minutes, then drew the drop cloth over it. Would it ever be finished? I wondered, frustrated. The kettle whistled, and I went to take it off the stove, measure tea into the pot, then pour the water into it. As I waited for it to brew, I wondered idly what had happened to my sketchbook and watercolors I'd taken to the beach that day. I'd made some good sketches, some that might be turned into salable watercolors. I frowned. How could they have just disappeared?

I took my tea over to the sofa and picked up the little book again. As I did, several narrow slips of paper fell out onto the coffee table. Apparently in the heat from the open fire the backing of the book had dried and loosened from its leather cover. Evidently these pieces had been placed between the cover and the front and back pages. There was something written on each one. I took them one by one and, puzzled, read each one, one after the other:

> "I do desire we may be better strangers . . ." *As You Like it?*
>
> "All the world's a stage/And all the men and women merely players;/They have their exits and their entrances;/And one man in his time plays many parts." *As You Like It*
>
> "Oh, how bitter a thing it is to look into happiness through another man's eyes." *As You Like It*
>
> "Tempt not a desperate man." *Romeo and Juliet*
>
> "The time of life is short;/To spend that shortness basely were too long." *Henry IV, Prt. II*
>
> "If you have tears—prepare to shed them now. Forever and forever, farewell—If we do not meet again, why we shall smile/If not, then this parting was well made." *Julius Caesar*
>
> "Pray, love, remember." *Hamlet*

Intrigued, I laid the slips of paper out in a row, and read them over and over. I felt a little guilty because in a way it seemed to be a series of messages, at least, the way I had arranged them. And yet, to what end?

I picked up the book and shook it gently, but no more slips of paper fell out. I looked closely at the binding of the back and front and noticed that the place they must have fallen from had been carefully slit open, then reglued.

A new thought struck me. Had the pieces of paper been hidden there?

What had at first seemed a kind of random jotting now began to take form and shape. Was this one side of a correspondence, an intimate exchange using a secret code of Shakespearean quotations to conduct a clandestine friendship, or more than that, a romance . . . a love affair?

Slowly, unrelated incidents began to sift through my mind—the argument I'd overheard between Dortha and an unknown person the first morning I was at Gull's Glen; the couple I'd seen walking on the beach in the moonlight; the mysterious figure in the hooded cape. Was Dortha involved in a secret relationship that now was causing her the extreme emotional stress she was obviously suffering?

CHAPTER 24

The next day I woke up to a sense of urgency, indefinable at first until I remembered that this was the day Ennis was due back from San Francisco.

With a kind of desperate optimism I hoped he had been able to have the dress repaired and was bringing it back in its restored condition.

The depressing fog still enfolded the cottage in its gray cocoon. I made myself coffee, debating whether or not to go up to the house for breakfast. I had gone up the night before to find I was dining alone. Justin had had his dinner on a tray upstairs with Dortha, and Bianca had stayed to dine with friends in Carmel after leaving Olivia in Pacific Grove. No one knew where Aaron was. Not that having a meal alone would have been any worse than eating with the sullen, silent boy, I thought. However, it was weird alone in that huge dining room, and I had finished quickly and started back to my cottage.

As I'd opened the door to go out, the fog was so thick and heavy I took the hooded cape from its hook beside the door, wrapped myself in it, and hurried through the woods back to the snug guest cottage.

Now, after two days of fog, I felt confined. With no work to do and no one to talk to, I was becoming nervous and edgy. I was anxious to hear from Ennis and kept watching the clock for his probable time of arrival back in Carmel.

But how would he to get in touch with me about the dress? With the Bradfords' unlisted phone number, and no excuse to come up on the property without revealing the errand, it would be difficult for him to return it openly or to get word to me.

Maybe I should walk down to the beach, and see if he was back yet. At least it would give me a reason to stretch my legs and get away from the confining cottage for a while.

As I wavered between indecision and action, a movement outside my window captured my immediate attention. Even in its strangeness there was a familiarity. I had seen this same figure pass by before, in the eerie light of dawn, wrapped in the cloak of darkness, and as now, shrouded in fog. Instinctively I ran to the window. But there was nothing to see. Gray emptiness stretched into the mist-hung trees. Could it have been an imagined vision?

No, it had come too often. I was too sensible a person to be influenced by my imagination. Impulsively I grabbed up the Irish cape, flung it around my shoulders, and ran outside.

The figure had come past my window from the direction of Rosalind's cottage, the last one of the three cottages toward the house through the woods. I quickened my step.

I was determined to find out who or what the ghostly apparition was, if not a figment of my imagination.

Suddenly the fog shifted and the figure came in sight again. I broke into a run, but like a phantom it was swallowed up in the mist, and I found myself alone, standing at the fork in the woods where the two paths crossed. One continued on to the main house, the other to the seawall and down to the beach. There was nothing in sight. I asked myself if it had been an illusion after all.

While I stood there frustrated, looking back and forth in both directions, a towering figure emerged through the mist coming from the house. His head down, striding forcefully along was Justin.

He seemed as startled to encounter me as I was at his sudden emergence out of the fog. I was struck again by Justin Bradford's appearance—the majestic head with its thick, wavy gray hair, the piercing eyes, the noble features, the tall lean body, attired now in a cowlneck sweater, and gray cord slacks. He could have been one of those commanding characters out of one of his novels.

"Miss Forrest!" he exclaimed. "I thought—for a moment—you were someone else. The cape, I guess," he said, and for the first time since I'd known him Justin seemed momentarily confused.

"You best be careful along this path in this pea soup," he commented. "I needed to get out for a while, clear my head a bit. My book—it's not going well at all. Sometimes I have to walk for hours to get things going again. Were you headed for the beach?"

I couldn't explain I'd run after a wisp of my imagination, so I nodded, and continued along the path with him, trying to match my shorter steps to his long strides.

Justin began to talk, almost as though he were thinking aloud.

"I've had writer's block before, but never this severe. There is such—turbulence, tension circulating around me.

It's impossible not to have it disturb my concentration, interfere with the smooth flow of work. It's all the fault of that damn—" Here he broke off, his voice harshened sharply. When I glanced sideways up at him, I was frightened to see how bitter and angry his expression was. There was a violence under the surface of this man which would be fearful indeed if it erupted.

As we neared the top of the steps leading down to the cove, I became extremely apprehensive. All the things I had heard about Justin flashed into my mind. Bianca had spoken of his terrible temper, Nell Sparrow of his irrational jealousy. Ennis even suspected him of murder!

For a few awful moments I was gripped in an intense premonition of danger. I slowed my steps, gradually coming to a stop. I looked down to where the surf was crashing against the cliffs and felt dizzy. It was a long way down. Suddenly I was rigid with terror and wished I had not walked out this far with Justin.

At the same time Justin had halted, presumably to let me precede him down the rickety stairs, simultaneously we both saw a slim, boyish figure with two dogs running along the beach below. Aaron and the Weimaraners!

"On second thought I don't think I'll walk on the beach this morning," Justin said abruptly. "I have had two explosive confrontations with my son in the last twenty-four hours, and I don't relish another one this soon."

With this Justin turned on his heels and walked away. I watched him disappear into the fog, and even though I told myself it was foolish, I sighed with relief.

How stressful it must be to live with a person of Justin's emotional temperament. No wonder Rosalind chafed under his obsessive love. How much more intimidated by him must the less stable Dortha be.

I glanced down at the beach again, but Aaron and the dogs had also been swallowed from sight by the fog. My own meetings with Aaron were the kind I'd rather avoid too. Besides, I didn't like the idea of him seeing me go to

Ennis Shelby's cottage. I had the uncomfortable feeling that Aaron might be the wraith in the woods I'd seen, with the unearthly ability to conceal himself around my cottage, spying on me, following me, fancying himself some kind of secret agent. Perhaps he was acting out a childish fantasy. Still, it was annoying.

By the time I reached the bottom of the steps, Ennis's cottage was barely visible in the ever-increasing fog. But as I got nearer, I was heartened to see lights shining from the windows. When I got to the front door, I heard music and I knocked confidently. Ennis was home, and I hoped he had good news about the dress.

I waited a reasonable time, and when he didn't come to the door, I knocked again.

Nothing happened. Maybe he was in the back and didn't hear me. After a few minutes more, I tried the doorknob, found it turned easily, so pushed it open. "Anyone home?" I called. No answer. I stepped inside and looked around.

He should be back before long, I told myself. Why else would he leave the lights on, the fire going, the stereo playing . . . ?

I tried calling his name again, and when there was no answer I had to conclude that Ennis wasn't there.

Knowing how anxious I was about Dortha's dress, I was sure he wouldn't mind if I waited. He had been so concerned, so helpful, I felt certain he would understand my coming into his empty house.

Although a cheerful fire crackled on the hearth, and all the lamps were lighted, there was an odd atmosphere in the cottage that gave me a feeling of apprehension. Maybe it was created by my own disquiet, or the oppressiveness of the fog outside and the sense of isolation it engendered.

I sat down gingerly on the edge of the sofa, anticipating that at any moment Ennis would walk in. But minutes went by, the stereo automatically turned off, and the clock ticking on the wall sounded very loud in the unnatural stillness.

I got up, restless, walked over to the window, and looked out, but by now the heavy fog had completely blotted out everything.

I turned back into the room. I might as well wait for him now that I was there, I decided. He couldn't object to that.

I went over to the sofa but felt too ill at ease to sit down. I picked up a pillow, absentmindedly plumped it and put it back. I looked around, unconsciously, searching for someplace Ennis might have hung the dress. My eyes lingered on the archway leading to the back of the cottage. Maybe . . .

I advanced cautiously, calling his name.

"Ennis! Ennis, are you here?"

I stood at the entrance of the narrow hallway leading to the rear of the house. There was a light shining from the door ajar at the end of the hall. I hesitated, listening for the sound of a shower or something that would indicate Ennis was in the cottage.

I took a few tentative steps farther. If he had brought the dress back, the logical place to hang it would probably be the bedroom. Would he mind if I took a look?

"Ennis!" I called once more, then walked down the short hallway.

Then I saw it.

Through the half-open door I could see into the bedroom and there, lighted like a museum masterpiece, hanging on the wall opposite the king-size bed, was the portrait of a woman. Transfixed at the doorway, I stared unbelievingly. With a kind of inner recognition, I knew it was the missing portrait of Rosalind, the one everyone thought stolen by Cole Burnham and destroyed with him in the fiery crash of his car.

Of course I had seen the photographs of Rosalind that Ennis had taken, but I think I would have known it was

Rosalind anyway. Although her strong features had been softened and idealized, the glorious mane of red-gold hair so like Olivia's, the vivid coloring described by Bianca and Nell Sparrow were all captured in the portrait. But more than that the artist had caught her seeking spirit. I had the feeling that she was impatiently holding that fluid pose, as if she could hardly wait to be up and off to some new venture or pursuit.

A few preliminary blue brush strokes suggesting the deep décolletage of a gown had been roughed in; the portrait was unfinished, but it had been beautifully and expensively framed.

I could not resist the urge to examine the portrait more closely. I stepped into the room, went over to the painting, and looked for a signature. It was unsigned, but I knew that this was the portrait Cole Burnham had been painting of Rosalind Bradford at the time of her death.

Suddenly I felt suffocated, breathless. Too many thoughts were rushing into my brain for me to sort them out, draw any sane conclusions. I gave a sweeping glance around the rest of the room, only to notice that, other than the portrait, there was no decoration.

Slowly I backed out of the room. Once in the hall, I walked quickly back into the living room, my heart fluttering as if I'd been running.

What did it mean, that shrinelike placement of Rosalind Bradford's stolen portrait in Ennis Shelby's bedroom? It was by rights Justin's. How had it come to be here? And why had Ennis given the impression in speaking of Rosalind that he was talking about his friend's tragic, star-crossed love affair? Had Jeff been right when he had suggested that Ennis was in love with Rosalind himself?

Should I leave now, I wondered. I stood uncertainly in the middle of the living room. I heard the eerie sound of a foghorn and shivered. By now it would be dark as well as foggy. Could I find my way alone back to the beach steps and back to the cottage at Gull's Glen?

I wrapped my arms around myself, and drew the Irish cape closer. Even in the warmth of the cottage, I felt suddenly cold. I went over to the fireplace and stood there, trying to stop my trembling. I turned my back to the fire to warm myself; at the same time my eyes glanced at the books on the coffee table. Somehow the assortment struck a chord in my memory—*The Life and Times of William Shakespeare;* another, *Elizabethan Poets;* still another, *Sonnets.* Automatically I picked up *Sonnets,* its cover design almost identical to the book I'd found on the ground near my cottage.

Inside was written, "To my own Dark Lady," and underneath it, "You are as haunting as twilight, elusive as evening shadows." And below that, "Not Will, dear heart, try to guess," then the initials E.S.

Slowly I turned the pages and saw that, as in the other book, this one was marked and underlined with little notations in the margins.

One by one pieces of the puzzle began to click into place. It began to add up. I hadn't asked Nell Sparrow who was in the Shakespeare Seven, but undoubtably Ennis had been, and obviously his relationship with Rosalind Bradford had been more than casual.

I don't know when the conviction that I was being watched began. It started as a kind of quiver in my neck and shoulders. It was not a conscious thing at all, simply intuitive. My hands turning the pages paused; I stood perfectly still. Then I heard Ennis's voice.

"So—you came after all."

I replaced the book on the table, and turned around.

At first Ennis's face betrayed nothing. It was curiously lacking in any discernible expression, and yet, instinctively, I knew it was not *me* he had meant. If I hadn't made it such a practice to study faces, I might have missed it. But there was a swift dilation of the pupils of his eyes, a slight twitch of his mouth that indicated surprise.

"The door was open—" I began..

"Why, of course, don't apologize. Didn't you know no one in Carmel ever locks their doors? A quaint native custom—but perhaps not too wise in some instances."

"I came about the dress. Were you able—?" The question hung unanswered between us.

"Will you have a brandy? It's just the sort of night for it," Ennis said, crossing over to the room divider and going behind it to bring out a bottle and two glasses.

I felt acutely uncomfortable.

"I hope you don't mind that I just walked in—"

"My dear Cam, I told you—"

"I know, but it's not the sort of thing I usually do. It was just that I was so anxious and the door was open." I halted. "I thought it would be all right if I came in and waited," I finished weakly.

Ennis poured the brandy carefully and said nothing.

"About the dress," I began again. "Were you able to locate the firm?"

Ennis was putting the glasses on a tray, getting out small paper napkins. Still he said nothing.

"Ennis," I said finally, "I feel terribly awkward. I think I've intruded. I think you're possibly angry with me."

He came over carrying the tray and set it down on the coffee table, having to move the books as he did so. If he knew I'd been looking at one, he gave no indication of it. He handed me a glass. I took it, still waiting for some answer, but he just stood there, swirling the brandy in the snifter, watching me.

I'm not sure what I felt then. The tension was strong; I felt apprehensive. I met his glance reluctantly.

Then Ennis smiled and shrugged. "It's not your fault, Cam. It's just that I was expecting someone else." He paused, letting that sink in. I felt my face flush. "That's why I left the lights on, the door open. The lady I'm expecting may turn up momentarily. I wouldn't want you to be embarrassed."

"Oh, I'll go right away," I said, putting down my untouched glass of brandy, and starting toward the door. Then, remembering why I'd come, I asked, "You didn't tell me about the dress."

Ennis shook his head regretfully. "I'm sorry, Cam. It's not repairable . . . ruined beyond salvaging."

Disappointment flooded through me. What would I tell the Bradfords? I managed to stammer, "Well, thanks for trying anyway, Ennis. I do appreciate your effort." I moved toward the door. Ennis followed. Then I saw something that started my heart thundering within me. I noticed, as though it had fallen between the wall and the stereo cabinet, a familiar canvas tote bag with the initials D.B. on it.

I tried to cover the shock I felt. Rosalind and Dortha, both of Justin's wives—and Ennis Shelby?

"That fog is awfully thick," Ennis said. "I better walk at least as far as the steps with you."

As if in answer to my silent pleas, we both heard the sound of barking, and peering through the grayish mass of fog, I saw the Bradford dogs and the tall, slim figure of Aaron.

Turning away from Ennis, I shouted desperately to the boy, "Aaron, Aaron, wait for me!"

"Thanks anyway, Ennis, for all your trouble," I called to him over my shoulder, stumbling almost blindly through the sand to where Aaron and the dogs had stopped on the dunes a few yards away.

I reached him and asked breathlessly, "Can I walk with you up to the house?"

He muttered something I took for assent, and I slogged after him through the loose sand, the dogs running alongside. I turned once to look back and saw—before the fog obliterated him from sight—Ennis silhouetted against the lighted interior of his cottage.

CHAPTER 25

When I gained the privacy of the guest cottage, I shut the door, locked it, and leaned against it, drawing in a shaky breath. At the intersection of the paths, Aaron had left me without a word and was quickly swallowed up in the darkness that had now descended. I had hurried back along the wooded path alone.

Once inside I was overwhelmed with my discoveries at Ennis Shelby's cottage. They had irrevocably changed my whole perception of the tragic situation at Gull's Glen, past and present. If Ennis Shelby, not Cole Burnham, had been Rosalind Bradford's lover, then he, not Bianca, was trying to destroy Justin, intimidate Dortha, and ruin their marriage! He had convinced himself Justin was responsible for Rosalind's death, and in some twisted way was out to vindicate her, to punish Justin because he had escaped the punishment Ennis must believe should have been legally administered. Ennis! I shook my head as if to clear it. The smooth-mannered, calmly objective, sincerely concerned friend—how I had been taken in by him!

I began to pace back and forth, holding onto myself as I shivered with nervousness. What was his motive? What did he hope to gain by these disruptive tactics? I stopped stock still in the midst of my pacing. The dress! Had Ennis been responsible for the ruined dress? Had he somehow gotten in this cottage while I was gone and arranged the damage himself, then pretended to help me by taking it to San Francisco to be repaired? No, it was too bizarre!

I was letting my imagination run wild.

The only way to settle it, to end my wild suspicions, was to confront Ennis with them.

I started for the door, but then the thought of the foggy night, going back down those treacherous steps, along that lonely stretch of beach to Ennis's cottage again stopped me.

Besides, what about Dortha?

Why was her bag at Ennis's? What connection could there possibly be between Dortha, Justin's new wife, and Ennis, his dead wife's lover?

Round and round in an endless circle my questions and answers tumbled one after the other in my mind.

I stopped my pacing suddenly. Who was Ennis expecting? I had the definite impression that when he first came in and found me there, my back to him, he had thought I was someone else. The cape, the hooded Irish cape that everyone and anyone could take and wear, had disguised my identity at first. What was it he had said when he first walked in? "So you came after all." There had evidently been some uncertainty as to whether or not the person would come.

Was he was expecting Dortha? Had she been there earlier without his knowledge, and for some unexplainable reason left her canvas tote bag?

Somehow I couldn't believe Dortha was having an affair with Ennis. I had come to know her pretty well during the sittings. She seemed genuinely in love with Justin.

Was she, then, in some way trying to protect Justin from Ennis? If so, how? What hold did Ennis have on Dortha? How was he threatening her?

How was I to find out the answers to any of these questions?

Had Ennis even tried to have the dress repaired? That, perhaps, was the telling question. If I were wrong in all my suspicions, the dress would be the clue. I had been so confused earlier at his cottage. Being caught, as it were, red-handed, I hadn't been thinking straight. I had merely accepted his statement that the damage was irreparable.

Determination to get to the core of this mystery galvanized me into action. Donning the cape again, I grabbed my car keys and went out into the fog-filled night.

I wouldn't risk the stairway to the beach, but there was another way down to Ennis's cottage. I would have to drive out to the highway, and take another winding road that provided access to his cottage and the other scattered cottages that fronted on the beach. I had to inch my way along, as the fog was heavy. As I went by the main house, I saw that only a few windows downstairs were lighted. I didn't know whether I was expected for dinner but I thought I had better leave word just in case. I braked quickly and ran up the steps to the house. When Rachel opened the door, I told her not to expect me for dinner. Her face registered dismay.

"Don't know what Cook's going to say, miss. Mr. Bradford took Miss Dortha to the doctor's this afternoon and they're not back. Miss Bianca phoned that she and Miss Olivia were staying for dinner in Pacific Grove another evening. Now you, miss."

"I'm sorry, Rachel, but something unexpected has come up." I started down the terrace steps. I really hadn't time to get involved in the domestic problems of the household. A sense of urgency pressed upon me.

For some reason I cut my engine and coasted for a few yards, then parked my car in the soft sand some distance from Ennis's cottage. My apprehension of what might be his reaction when I confronted him with my suspicions momentarily daunted me. I sat for a few minutes, my hands gripping the steering wheel, my heart pumping rapidly, gathering up my courage. These were questions that had to be answered, questions I had to ask. Finally I got out of the car, closing the door quietly behind me.

Ennis's Ferrari was parked in the carport. Silently I went around to the driver's side and looked in the window. I tried the door but it was locked. I got out the pocket flashlight I carried in my purse and shined it into the back of the car. There, I thought, was my proof. The box in which I had placed the ruined red dress was still there, wrapped and tied just as I had given it to Ennis three days before. It did not look as if it had been moved or unwrapped.

I clicked off the light, then walked along the side of the cottage toward the front door, rehearsing the indignant demand for an explanation I was going to make of Ennis.

But just outside the front door I was halted by the sound of angry voices raised in loud argument.

Ordinarily it might have been difficult to hear what was being said inside over the sound of the surf. But for some reason the heavy fog acted as an insulator, shutting out the noise of the ocean that otherwise might have drowned out the voices.

What I heard stopped me cold.

"What will you take in exchange for those pictures?"

Without doubt that was Dortha Bradford's voice, but pitched at a frenzied height I'd never heard before.

I could barely hear the reply, but her reaction came through to me clearly.

"You beast! You vindictive, ruthless beast! If you can't be happy yourself, you won't allow anyone else to be! What has Justin ever done to you to make you hate him so? To use me to hurt him!"

The answer, evidently spoken in a low tone, was inaudible to me, even though by this time I had pressed my ear to the door and was listening unashamedly.

"That's no reason!" I heard Dortha say. "All that happened a long time ago. It has nothing to do with me, or Justin, for that matter. He was not responsible for Rosalind's death, no matter what you say! I know all about it. He kept nothing from me. He told me before we were married. And those pictures—you know why I posed for them. I was young and stupid and ambitious—and broke and hungry! I didn't know any better than to believe that they were necessary for me to get modeling jobs. And what about you? You're no better than he was! You worked for him, didn't you? Don't tell me your excuse was better than mine. You were struggling to get ahead. We all were in those days!" Her voice took on a pleading note. "Ennis, for old times' sake, give me those pictures. We were friends once. Can't we—"

There was a retort, and some more exchanges I couldn't hear, then Dortha's voice rose again.

"You can't want money. But if you do, I'll get it for you. Anything! Just don't, I beg you, go to Justin. He's suffered enough."

There were more words exchanged, then Dortha's voice came loud and clear. "Whatever you call it, it's blackmail, extortion! That's a crime, you know!"

I was really frightened now. Dortha was on dangerous ground. The words I'd found on one of those slips of paper that had fallen from the loosened binding of the book I'd found had read, "Do not tempt a desperate man." They flashed into my mind then. Dortha was doing just that. I had a premonition of enormous danger.

I had no time to anticipate what to do next, for at that moment I heard footsteps approaching and had only a minute to jump back and crouch behind the huge bushes beside the front door just as it burst open and someone rushed out.

I could only guess it was Dortha.

I huddled there, shivering uncontrollably, wondering what would happen next. There passed a few agonizingly long minutes, then the front door closed, leaving me in total darkness.

CHAPTER 26

I don't know how much time passed. It seemed ages. I dared not move, afraid to risk giving myself away by rustling a bush or making a sound that would alert Ennis to my presence. Hardly breathing, I could only allow myself the merest easement of muscle, the slightest shifting of my cramped position. It was torture as I remained there for what seemed an endless length of time, silent and motionless, waiting for I knew not what to happen.

Then suddenly the front door swung open and a shaft of light narrowly missed revealing me as I ducked even lower. Then the rush of footsteps sounded on the wooden porch. I felt the stirring of air as Ennis ran past me. Slowly I raised myself, flexing my arms. I heard the roar of the powerful engine of his Italian sports car, the gritty sound of spraying gravel and sand as his wheels spun for a few seconds before the noise of his motor speeding down the road told me he'd left.

I got up stiffly, letting out my breath, steadying myself against the rough shingles of the house. The front door he had slammed after him had not caught and now it swung open.

I looked at it, torn between two courses of action. I could leave now, get away safely, no one being the wiser. But something compelled me to do otherwise. I liked Dortha Bradford. I pitied her and longed for her to be happy. I abhorred what I had overheard. For some twisted reason Ennis was blackmailing Dortha to settle some vendetta with Justin. It was wrong and vicious, and it made me angry.

But what could I possibly do?

Without any real plan, I acted on pure instinct. They had argued about some pictures—photographs. Some photographs that Dortha was ashamed of and that Ennis was threatening to show Justin. Since whatever the deal was had not been settled between them, the logical conclusion was that the photographs were still in Ennis's possession. They must be in his cottage somewhere.

With more speed than caution I went inside. I closed the door behind me and looked around frantically. If I were Ennis, where would I hide incriminating pictures I was going to use to blackmail someone?

I wracked my brain, trying to recall the methods used in all the spy stories and cloak and dagger movies I'd seen.

Sometimes people hid things in the most obvious places, believing searchers would think them too simple and never look there. So I started by pulling out the several thick volumes of photograph albums Ennis kept on the lower shelves of the bookcase.

I had seen them the night I'd had dinner here. He had brought some of them out and we'd sat together on the sofa looking at them. Remembering that night, I shook my head. It seemed incredible that the civilized, charming, talented man whose skill with a camera was pure art could be capable of the basest kind of criminal exploitation—blackmail! And on someone as helpless and vulnerable as Dortha. I could hardly believe it. If I had not overheard part of their conversation myself, it would have seemed impossible.

I dragged out the heavy albums and spread them helter-skelter on the floor, turning the pages one by one, running my hand behind some of the mats to see if some were slipped behind.

Then I came across another startling discovery. Among the albums I found two of Rosalind's scrapbooks, the ones Bianca kept in the cottage. How had Ennis got them? Had he been the prowler I'd seen the other night, when he was supposed to be in San Francisco? I remembered that the figure had seemed to be carrying something heavy. The next day I'd found the book of Shakespeare with the secret messages. Ennis stealing mementos of his dead love? But how had he got in? Perhaps the same key fit all the cottages, and he had a duplicate made from Cole Burnham's. I didn't have time to ponder all the complexities of Ennis's actions. I had to find those pictures of Dortha.

My feeling of urgency mounted. I had no idea where Ennis had gone or how soon he could return. I had to find those pictures and get them to Dortha. Frustrated, I slammed the albums shut and shoved them back into the lower shelves of the bookcase, stood up, and looked around the room for other possible hiding places. Seeing a sheaf of large manila envelopes piled on the desk, I went over to them and flipped through them. They were marked by size and subject and a quick undoing of each clasp and quicker look inside showed that they were not what I was hoping to find.

I don't know when the idea of Rosalind's portrait hit me, but as soon as it did, I ran down the narrow hall and into the bedroom. I knew that the back of a framed canvas usually provides a few inches of space that could make a perfect hiding place. The portrait was nearly full length, so the frame was very large and heavy. It was extremely awkward trying to shift it so that I could get my hand behind it and feel for any hidden package.

With one hand I managed to inch the bottom part of the frame away from the wall enough to squeeze my fingers up and under. I felt a rush of excitement as I touched a wedge of paper. Frantically I pried at the tape that held the thick paper to the wood edge of the frame. I felt it tear loose a little, and breathing heavily from the effort of holding the heavy frame, I worked the tape off. I was so completely absorbed in my struggle that I lost track of time. Just as the paper came loose and slithered down to the floor, I became aware, subliminally, that I was no longer alone.

The door behind me opened. I swung around, my heart thundering.

Ennis stood there, looking steadily at me, his own face betraying no emotion.

I had a sense of unreality. I was taut with nervousness, chilled with apprehension. Fear surged up inside me, squeezing the breath out of me, tightening itself like unseen hands gripping my throat. I tried to swallow, to wet my dry lips. I found I was immobilized. I simply stood there staring at him in disbelief.

Then at last he broke the unnatural silence.

"What the hell do you think you're doing?" he demanded in an icy tone.

I found I could not speak.

He repeated the question in a deadly even voice.

Beneath the cool exterior he was attempting to project I felt certain an inner rage seethed. All my courage deserted me. I threw out my hands in a kind of helpless gesture. What was there to say? I'd been caught red-handed.

"What were you looking for?" he asked, his eyes flicking over me and beyond to the picture I had been trying in vain to dislodge.

I knew there was no use lying.

"The photographs you've been threatening Dortha Bradford with."

He gave a short, ugly laugh. "What difference could that possibly make to you?"

"Because I like Dortha, and I think it's a despicable thing you're doing."

"You don't know her," he said, shrugging. "Dortha and I go back a long way. To New York when we were both struggling to get a start. She as a model. I had a menial job as an assistant to a photographer. Don't waste your sympathy on Dortha Waldren—she's a dime-a-dozen little opportunist. She's nothing." His voice became rough, bitter. "She couldn't make it as a model, so she tried to marry money. But she picked the wrong man. I have a score to settle with Justin Bradford. Dortha provided me with the means to do it." Ennis's eyes had narrowed, his mouth distorted in a snarl. "This has nothing to do with you, Cam, so why don't you just quit while you're ahead? Don't interfere in something that's none of your business."

But it was too late for that. What Ennis didn't know was that my thrusting fingers had found the slim packet taped to the back of the portrait, that I was sure I'd found the pictures.

How could I buy some time, distract him enough so that I could retrieve the small envelope I was sure contained the pictures from where they had fallen. I felt them with my foot in the deep shag rug. If I could just keep eye contact with Ennis, slide them under the bed, then, maybe . . .

"Come on, Cam, leave well enough alone. I have other things to do tonight besides argue with you." Ennis's voice had an edge to it now. I felt a tremor in my legs as the anticipation of fear of what might happen stirred within me. Still, I'd come this far. I was determined to help Dortha. No matter about her past, she deserved happiness now. Ennis's personal revenge against Justin for the suspected death of Rosalind should not damage her.

"Why did you let everyone think it was Cole who was in love with Rosalind?" I asked him, trying to keep my voice from trembling.

His eyes widened, then the pupils dilated. A wild kind of look came into his face, and I held my breath. In that split second I saw that Ennis's urbanity was a veneer. He had the capacity to turn savage.

I gauged the distance to the door, the probability of my making it through the hall and living room and outside before he could catch me. He had moved gradually as we talked to the center of the room exactly opposite me, where I stood in front of the portrait of Rosalind. If I made a run for it, pulling the bedroom door shut behind me, I might just make it.

In one swift movement I dropped to my knees, picked up the small envelope, sprinted to the door, grabbed the knob, and slammed it as I passed through, then rushed down the hallway. Then I stumbled, pitching forward, my hands plunging ahead of me still clutching the envelope. As I staggered to my knees, I felt my arm wrenched backward, sending a ferocious pain splitting through it to my shoulder. My wrist was twisted, and I heard myself scream. The envelope was torn out of my grasp.

"That was a stupid thing to do," Ennis said breathlessly. "Now get up and get out of here." He yanked me roughly to my feet.

He gave me a hard push between my shoulder blades out into the living room.

I made one last effort. "What good will it do to ruin Dortha's marriage, create a scandal?" The pain in my arm must have made me mad to pursue this, but maybe I figured the worst had already happened. I'd failed to get the photos.

Ennis turned on me savagely.

"Do you know what it's like to love someone you can't have. We almost made it, Rosalind and I. She was finally convinced she couldn't go on living with Justin while loving me. His possessiveness was becoming too much. She was like a prisoner. I loved her enough to want her to be free. Sure, we used Cole as a cover. He was my friend, he was willing to take messages between us, arrange meetings. When he was supposed to be painting her, she would come down here and we'd have a few hours together, undisturbed. Cole had made it a requisite of his taking the commission to paint her that no one would interupt the hours of the sittings. But that sister of hers . . . so afraid that she'd lose her security, her position. She liked living in the luxury Justin's success provided. She'd had enough of one-night bookings, cheap hotels, sleazy theaters, when she traveled with Rosalind as an aspiring actress. She began to suspect, spy on her. Then the night I'd finally persuaded Rosalind to go away with me, it happened."

Ennis had gone over to the room divider, picked up a decanter, and poured himself a drink. His voice was ragged as he continued.

"I had told her that most courts would award her custody of her children. She was afraid that Justin could somehow keep her from having them.

"I'm sure Bianca went to Justin and told him her suspicions. But it was Cole they suspected, not me. That's when Justin confronted Cole, threw him off the property. I knew we had to act then. We planned to leave together that night."

Ennis's hand shook as he raised the glass and took a swallow.

"I know Rosalind was coming to me. Justin must have caught her as she was leaving. They quarreled. His insane temper—" Ennis's voice broke. He slumped against the counter, shaking his head, one hand shielding his face.

I don't know how many minutes went by. I saw a shudder pass over Ennis's whole body, and I realized he was trying to regain his composure.

"You loved her very much, didn't you?" I asked after a long while.

He straightened up slowly, nodded, took up his glass again.

"She was everything to me. Everything."

"That's why you took the painting?"

"Yes. It was the only thing I had of her. It was the way she looked those last weeks when we were so much in love. I had to have it." He paused. "There's never been anyone else in my life." His face hardened. "All these years I've been trying to find some way to get back at Justin Bradford. Then I ran into Dortha right here in Carmel, only a few weeks ago. I knew I had my key. I had to go up to

San Francisco to my studio, search through all my old files to find those shots of her, those cheesecake photos, the kind they used to use on calendars. Now I guess I could get plenty selling them. Imagine the notoriety—the highly respectable, best-selling author's wife as a centerfold!" He gave a brief, harsh laugh.

I took a few steps toward him and said in a low voice, "You don't want to do this awful thing, Ennis."

"The hell I don't! It's no more than he deserves!"

"But what about Dortha? She never did anything to hurt you."

"Just the same—" he retorted defensively, taking another sip of his drink. "Two people are dead, for God's sake!" he cried. "Somebody's got to pay for that." Ennis's voice broke harshly.

"But why Dortha, Ennis? She had nothing to do with any of this. She didn't even know Justin until a few months ago. I can't believe you want to destroy her happiness because of a tragic accident. She isn't to blame." Ennis seemed to be listening impassively until I made my final attempt to sway him. "What would Rosalind think of your doing it, Ennis?" I asked softly. "Is that any way to memorialize your love for her?"

An expression of pain came into Ennis's eyes, and he turned away from me, leaning his head against the mantelpiece.

A silence fell and lengthened. I thought I'd said too much. My whole body tensed, waiting for some reaction.

Then he reached into the inside pocket of his corduroy jacket, drew out the brown manila envelope, held it for a few minutes, then pulled out a gold cylindrical lighter and flicked it. As I watched him, he set fire to the envelope. It burst into a flaming pyramid, and he tossed it into the huge conch shell to shrivel into a pile of ashes.

CHAPTER 27

It seemed hours later when I walked into the guest cottage and straight into Jeff Maxwell's arms. My surprise merged into a tremendous sense of security. I felt myself tremble, and his arms tightened. We stood there for a long moment, holding each other. Then he said softly, "Well, maybe it was worth being stood up for this."

I looked up at him, momentarily puzzled. Strangely enough, I hadn't questioned his being there.

"What do you mean?" I asked.

"We had a dinner date tonight, remember? They said up at the house it would be all right for me to wait for you down here." He held me away from him and studied my face. "Hey, is something wrong? Did something happen to upset you?"

I sighed. "Oh, Jeff, there's so much to tell you, to explain."

"Come on, sit down," he said, leading me over to the couch in front of the fireplace where a cheerful blaze was burning. "Is there anything around here to drink? You look as though you could use something."

"On the table over there," I directed him shakily, indicating the decanter of sherry.

While I waited, I held out cold hands to the warmth of the fire.

In a minute Jeff was back. He put a glass of sherry into my numb hand.

"Now tell me," he said firmly.

After I'd poured out the whole incredible story, I said, "I'll have to tell Dortha that she hasn't anything more to fear from Ennis."

"We'll go up together," Jeff said, rising.

"Thanks," I said gratefully.

His arm around me was comforting as we took the wooded path up to the house.

Rachel let us in and said Justin and Dortha were in the library. Justin rose to greet us as Rachel announced us. I looked over at Dortha. She looked pale and her eyes were red-rimmed from weeping, yet there was a curious calmness about both of them.

"I don't really know how to begin," I said hesitantly. Then, little by little, I told them what I'd begun to suspect about Ennis, about the ruined dress, about going to his cottage and overhearing the conversation between him and Dortha, and finally about the burning of the photographs. All the time I was talking, Justin and Dortha listened. At one point Dortha's head dropped, and she covered her face with her hands. Justin immediately put an arm protectively around her slim shoulders. Neither of them interrupted or said a word until I was finished.

"And he has the portrait everyone thought stolen." I looked directly at Justin as I spoke, not knowing how much that would mean to him.

He nodded. "Of course we all thought Cole was the one," he said quietly. He stood up and came over to me, taking both my hands. "Cam, I don't know how we can adequately thank you. But I must tell you that after leaving Ennis's cottage earlier this evening, Dortha came to me and told me his whole sordid plot. We're not going to let him get away with it. I was going to my attorney tomorrow. Blackmail is a crime and even the threat of it is legally punishable." Justin paused. "As a writer, I should know how human behavior is most often motivated by mistaken attitudes, wrong ideas—what a twisted emotion love can become. No doubt Ennis felt he was justified if he honestly believed I had caused Rosalind's death. Cam, I feel you have the right to know the truth.

The truth is that I was not responsible for her death. No one was. Although . . ."

He went over to the fireplace, put one arm out, and leaned against the mantelpiece for a few minutes before continuing to speak.

"Before I tell you what really happened the night Rosalind died, I must ask both of you for absolute confidentiality. There is nothing to be gained at this point by any blame being leveled. The person most directly responsible—although not intentionally so—has already suffered, and has been punished enough."

Jeff and I both murmured our assent and Justin continued. "Bianca had been suspicious for some time that Rosalind was involved with someone else—although, and this I have never revealed to another living soul, that night Rosalind had left a letter to me in which she assured me that her affection for me and our children was deep, unchanged, even though she found the passion she felt for this other person too strong for her to withstand any longer, she asked me to forgive her." Justin passed his hand across his forehead, sighed, and went on. "As I said, Bianca's suspicions centered on Cole and that night she followed Rosalind along the seawall after Rosalind had slipped away from the house to go to Ennis's cottage. It seems they had already made preparations to go away together that night. Anyway, Bianca caught up with Rosalind and they quarreled violently. Bianca tried to stop her—physically. As they struggled at the top of the beach steps, Rosalind lost her balance—" Justin's voice faltered "—and fell to her death."

The room was unnaturally still as we all waited for Justin to go on. Jeff's hand found mine and gave it a reassuring squeeze.

"Horrified, Bianca was unable to get to Rosalind in the dark, and came running back to the house to me, almost hysterical. When we found Rosalind, it was too late. Her neck was broken. She must have died instantly. While we waited for Ted Sparrow and the ambulance to come, Bianca and I decided that since Rosalind was dead there was no use letting a scandal erupt about the circumstances. That would only give those notorious newspapers a headline to sell their trash and hurt the children. It was Rosalind's habit to often walk at night, probably on those very walks, she met Ennis—" Justin sighed again. "And this is what we told the police investigating the accident. When, later, Cole Burnham, probably instigated by Ennis Shelby, brought accusations against me, Bianca came to my defense.

"Shortly after the inquest Bianca suffered a complete collapse. She had to be hospitalized for several months. I took the children with me to Switzerland while she was in the sanitorium. The doctors there told me she had recovered—except for what they termed traumatic amnesia. Her part in Rosalind's death was totally wiped out of her memory. It was the only way she could bear to go on living, so her subconscious mind forgot it. She was always rather jealous and hostile toward me, falsely blaming me for Rosalind giving up a promising film career. Actually Rosalind gave it up quite willingly. She wanted a home and family at the time we married. She told me over and over it was Bianca, perhaps wanting to live vicariously through Rosalind, who had pushed her into acting.

"Rosalind told me she had come to hate the theatrical life and though, later, domesticity may have palled, at the time we married she was not the dedicated actress Bianca makes her out to be. It's ironic, isn't it, how we deceive ourselves and fail to communicate to others?"

Jeff stayed with me only long enough to see me safely to the cottage. "You're exhausted," he said. "Get a good night's sleep, and I'll see you tomorrow." He held me for a minute, then kissed me lightly.

He was right, and I should have been able to go right to sleep. But I was too stimulated by all the events of the day.

I could still see Dortha's face as she told of the unexpected meeting with Ennis in Carmel, her shock when she realized he intended to shatter her newfound happiness. Then, she told of her desperate search of his beach house to find the incriminating evidence. The night she had fallen, spraining her ankle, was a last try at unearthing them before he took them to Justin.

She had broken down in telling about it and Justin had immediately tried to quiet her sobs by telling her it didn't made any difference in the way he felt about her. It was plain to see that Ennis was wrong about Dortha, I thought. She and Justin genuinely loved each other. I hoped their future together would be happier now.

CHAPTER 28

I awoke to the patter of light rain and the sound of someone moving about in the living room. I slipped on my robe and looked out of the bedroom door to see Rachel getting a fire started.

"Good morning, miss," she greeted me cheerfully. "I've brought down fresh blueberry muffins for your breakfast. Mr. Bradford sent word he would be down in about an hour."

When Justin arrived, I knew he had something important on his mind. After I poured both of us coffee, he got right to the point.

"Cam, I've decided Dortha and I need to get away from here for a while. Maybe it was a mistake to come back here. Nevertheless, I've got a fair start on my book, and I'm going to take some time off and get to know my children again. I've talked to Bianca and she has been invited to go with friends to the Shakespeare Theater in Ashland, Oregon, for a month. So I think we'll just close Gull's Glen for a while." He took a check out of his pocket and handed it to me.

I looked at it and nearly gasped at the amount.

"But the portrait—the one you wanted in the red dress—it isn't finished!" I protested.

He shook his head.

"Maybe it wasn't meant to be. Anyway, Dortha likes the other one you did of her better, and so that's the one we'll buy."

When I looked at the amount of the check Justin handed me, I saw that it was twice what I charged for one finished portrait. When I protested, Justin simply refused to discuss it.

"Besides, Cam, we could never repay you for what you went through for us. We're both so grateful. I only wish your stay at Gull's Glen had been a more peaceful, happier one."

Of course Justin did not know about my relationship with Jeff, which in a way was just as unfinished as my portrait of Dortha.

I was expecting Jeff to come that evening so we could spend my last evening at Gull's Glen together. I felt sure he was going to ask me for a commitment, and I wasn't completely sure I was ready to make one.

This was very much on my mind that afternoon as I packed my car in preparation for leaving the following morning. Olivia had been with me for hours to help, but for the most part she had simply watched and chattered. She was very excited about her father's plans to go to Europe. Like the little chameleon she was, she seemed to have changed her attitude toward Dortha drastically.

"You know, Dortha was a model and she's promised to teach me all those model tricks, like standing, turning, and all that. It's very important for an actress to know how to move gracefully, you know. And I am going to be an actress. My father actually agreed that I could take dramatics this year at school. Imagine!"

Olivia was so self-absorbed that I could almost tune her out and concentrate on my own thoughts—that is, until she mentioned Aaron. Then my ears pricked up.

"Do you know what he's been doing all this time when he sneaked off by himself, Cam? He's been painting! I had to take some clean clothes up to his room for Aunt Bianca this morning for him to pack, and I saw some canvases. There pretty good, too. Of birds mostly and the ocean, stuff like that. I never knew he was even interested in painting before. Well, he came in and found me looking at them and got real mad." She shrugged and then immediately launched into her plans to go with Dortha into San Francisco for a shopping trip before they left for Europe. "She knows all about fashion and style, you know," she told me importantly.

For the first time it dawned on me who had taken my sketch pads and brushes that had so mysteriously disappeared. Maybe Aaron had done it initially just to be spiteful and then become interested and started to use them. I remembered Jeff telling me about him coming to the store and checking on the prices of brushes and paints. Well, that cleared that mystery up, I thought.

I might have just written the whole thing off if I hadn't later come across a grubby envelope on the windshield of my VW. It had been pushed under the wipers. Curiously I opened it and found some crumpled dollar bills and some change. There was a note, too, scrawled in a boyish hand!

"Sorry about taking your stuff. Hope this will cover the cost of what I took. It was a crazy kid thing to do." The note wasn't signed.

I hoped Aaron had not repaid me just because he suspected Olivia would tell on him. I hoped he was genuinely sorry, but who could tell with Aaron? Maybe getting started in something creative would help the boy. All I could do was wish him well.

Dortha was the last person at Gull's Glen to come and tell me good-bye. Bianca had been down earlier and given me as cool a farewell as her welcome had been. But Dortha, released from all her haunting fears, was openly friendly and regretful of all the problems she had caused with the portrait.

She gave me a lovely silver pin in the shape of a palette as a parting gift. Then she hugged me and said, "I'll never forget what you did for me, Cam." Her lovely eyes were bright with tears. "I'm sorry I wasn't a more cooperative model."

Now there was one more good-bye to say.

Jeff and I had dinner in a charming restaurant tucked away in one of the hidden courts in Carmel. Its air of intimacy was enhanced by the dark wood decor, old brick, tables for two set in small alcoves and checked tablecloths on which candles in wine bottles dripped colored wax. The waiter who served us seemed to anticipate our every need. Jeff looked at me over the rim of his wineglass and said for the second time, "I wish you weren't going."

"I think we've had this conversation before," I said, smiling. "You know I've got everything set and now with what Justin paid me I won't have to worry about finances until fall."

"Then what?"

"Then," I said slowly, "I guess I'll go back to teaching."

"There is an alternative," Jeff said. "You know I love you." He covered my hand with his. "I honestly love you. What more could an artist want but to live in Carmel and get all her paintings framed for free?" he asked teasingly.

I looked at him and smiled. "I really can't think of any argument to that," I said.

"Well, then—" Jeff grinned broadly.

"Give me a little time, Jeff," I asked quietly.

"All the time you want—within reason, of course," he answered.

After dinner we drove back to Gull's Glen to the guest

cottage. It was late by then, and I wanted to get an early start in the morning, so I didn't ask Jeff in. We stood on the doorstep, his arms around my waist, reluctant to really say good-bye.

"I wish you weren't going," he said for the third time.

"But I've still got the rest of the summer to paint. You know I want to do enough work to have a full portfolio to take to one of the galleries in San Francisco."

"There's a gallery here. You can have a one-woman show any time," Jeff reminded me.

"Jeff!" I said in mock exasperation, "I thought you understood."

"I do understand, only—" and he drew me into his arms. "Don't be gone long."

Jeff's arms stayed around me, holding me close. Suddenly it felt wonderfully right to be there. I realized his was a very special kind of love. The love Jeff offered made me feel both cherished and free. It was the kind of love that would let me be my own person, yet his, too.

I lifted my face for his kiss.

"It will be just until the end of summer," I murmured after a long while.

"Promise?" he asked.

"Yes." It was the easiest promise I ever made.

"In September, then. In the fall Carmel is the best place to be."

I smiled up at him happily, knowing that from now on, wherever Jeff was would be the best place for me.